Bayside

A Novel

BAYSIDE

W.H. Hyland

Author's Note

With the exception of municipalities, public figures, and some educational institutions, the places, people, and events pertinent to this story are both composites of the author's personal experience and fictional portrayals from his imagination. Any allusions and similarities to real-life, living or dead, are creative in nature or coincidental. In addition, any trademarks, service marks, product names, or named features are assumed to be the property of their respective owners and are used only for reference. If any of these terms are used, no endorsement is implied. Except for review purposes, the reproduction of this book, in whole or part, electronically or mechanically, constitutes a copyright violation.

Address permissions and review inquiries to sportlandmedia@gmail.com.

Written and Edited by: William H. Hyland, Sportland Media
Cover Art: Canva stock, compiled by William H. Hyland
Author Photo: Summer Hyland

<u>Follow the Author on Social Media</u>

X/Twitter: @willhyland

Instagram: @whhylandwrites

To My Family

Prologue

Where I live, news as big as what happened earlier this year comes with a disturbing sense of fascination from the outside: a place like ours heralded for its charm and authenticity overtaken by a desire to spin that same place as untamed and yet still miraged. You see, when Maine gets any sort of national media coverage, even some folks up here get caught up in the newly reported story rather than what actually happened, almost as if to relish in the attention to which our state only receives when a Zumba studio becomes a brothel or when a high school mascot is renamed. Of course, it is later when Maine becomes the punchline again, a place where overalled cousins get married on a blueberry farm, officiated by Stephen King and a pet moose.

Though a high crime and betrayal of this magnitude was unlike anything most Mainers had seen within our borders. It unearthed some of the growing insecurities that locals had about public safety and confidence in their fellow man. Crime was always something that happened far away from Maine or in seemingly less-desirable parts of the state, not where cousins Sally and Timmy come for sailing camp. No. Not ever.

Further, it opened up the same national scrutiny I mentioned, only multiplied exponentially. If Fox News *and* CNN are questioning the sanctity and stability of your region's reputation, then you are in bigger trouble than you thought, I imagined. And, if a *New York Times* columnist is writing an op-ed on why tourists should avoid

Maine next summer rather than why they should drop everything and go, then it spelled disaster. Our local body politic was usually defined by a Republican being too liberal and a Democrat being too conservative, but never by a cable television opening monologue.

Nevertheless, we Mainers are used to explaining a lot of things, just not why something like this could happen. We're used to weaving a verbal geographic web for our out-of-state friends, telling them we indeed live a three-hour drive from where they once stayed in a beachside cottage. What we're not used to is having our dirty laundry aired in the national conversation.

Of course, this wasn't the only crime to happen in Vacationland over the past year, but it somehow became the most interesting to those inside and outside our borders. Homicides and burglaries had been increasing year by year yet somehow all of that was lost when compared to other states, not surprisingly. After all, Maine's sturdy reputation as a tourist haven was authentically constructed because the drugs, murders, and sex scandals had been limited to old mill towns off the beaten path or city neighborhoods that everyone already wished to ignore. To the outsiders, our other tragedies to date were swept up in national polarization and soon forgotten. They saw those events as spokes in a wheel of news cycles, and some went on their way while our citizens reeled. But this time, for those on the outside, it wasn't merely a token for continuing national debate. Rather, its conclusion was the focus of a weeks-long media frenzy that descended upon sleepy Maine. I feared that our carefully woven postcard image was in greater peril than ever.

As for me, I too was in a front-row seat, but completely by chance. As a young man, I had lived a normal life here on the coast of

Maine, near the small village of Bayside, and every other major news event of my childhood took place in some far-off land on a television screen. But as fate would have it, I not only found myself on the front lines of this mystery but also directly involved in its investigation. So believe me when I say that such fascination, scrutiny, and skepticism from near and far do not result in the kind of fame I had hoped for. Even after a few short months, I sadly dread returning home for the holiday break from college, knowing that some reporter or true crime superfan would have left messages with my folks, wanting to talk about this disturbing experience.

And yet with all that, this story began at the most ordinary of places, the Rockland, Maine branch of the Bureau of Motor Vehicles.

***

It had been fifty minutes already. Looking around, I saw torn people. Some old, some young. Some rich, some poor. Some eager, some complacent. Squeaky chair fidgeters and those glued to their phones. I shuffled my hat and my backpack and peered at the wall, contemplating if it was worth it or not to get out my headphones. I still had the old kind, where you had to plug them into your phone. Most people here did too.

I had just returned home from my junior year at Dartmouth College. Not many kids from my town made it out of Waldo, Lincoln, or Knox counties - also known as the Midcoast - let alone to the Ivy League. People I knew in Hanover were puzzled at that concept, but I embraced it. We were misunderstood by the greater population. Driven by loyalty to place and pride in our work ethic. Folks around the rest of America probably thought we were a bunch of hillbillies, who did not enjoy anything beyond lobster, Moxie, and coffee brandy. Their perceived ideas of Mainers often rested with those who lived in glorious capes and walked their dog on brick sidewalks. Of course, those folks are Mainers too, but not everyone resided in that luxury. Despite living just minutes from the ocean, my family had modest roots. But still, it was difficult for me to fit in with either group, if I am being honest. Some friends of mine lived in trailers, others went skiing every winter weekend over in the Carrabassett Valley. Clear as day though was the idea that even though this region had its share of haves and have-nots, we were *all* trying to leave our friends and family better off than ourselves.

"Now serving number 128," the loudspeaker read. After almost an hour, my time had come. I approached the counter to get my driver's license renewed.

"Name please," said the woman working the counter.

"Bakeman," I replied. "William Robert Bakeman."

One

My friends called me Billy, or, if they wanted to get me rattled, Billy Bob. I was to be twenty-two later this year, and, for the first time since leaving for Dartmouth after high school, I was feeling confident about my future. My past, however, was still nothing to scoff at.

I was born and spent all of my childhood here in the Penobscot Bay region of Maine, a place known for its quaintness and natural beauty. I am incredibly lucky to have grown up in this place. When I describe its location to those who hail from elsewhere, I usually just say "It's the big gap in the coast of Maine if you were to look at a map." However, I am unsure if they'd admit whether or not they understood that either.

More specifically, I was born in Belfast at one of the regional hospitals. Our home near Bayside Village was a part of the Town of Northport. Kids like me who lived in Northport almost always went to high school in Belfast.

Belfast is also where my parents work, where we go shopping, and where a lot of local commerce takes place. For most of my life, it had been the real epicenter of daily and weekly activity. In many ways, the complex municipal ecosystem - where no two towns were alike nor that different, and where you knew people from every town - was a key driver in local identity. Folks described themselves as being from "Waldo County" or the "Midcoast" as often as they labeled themselves residents of any particular town.

But like any place, there were still rich towns and poorer towns. Belfast was more blue-collar than nearby Camden, but Northport, and specifically our Bayside Village within it, close to my house and the golf club, were seasonally more affluent. My family was halfway decent financially, and probably still seen as "rich" by some in the area who knew us. Dad ran a local tax filing service and Mom was now the principal at the high school I once attended. My Ivy League admission was a ticket to join my uncle though, I hoped. He was an attorney in Camden and made pretty good money.

I studied government but planned to go to law school after graduation next spring. My uncle hired me as an intern this summer at his firm, Bakeman & Courtier. It was probably peanuts compared to what my classmates were landing with Dartmouth alumni, but it was a start.

Uncle Jack, my dad's older brother, was well-respected in the community and had impressive connections all over New England and the Canadian Maritimes. He was a stakeholder in many industries like lobstering, fishing, agriculture, and logistics. Jack was a skilled mariner and oceanographer too on the side. Business leaders relied on his firm for counsel, and thus, it was a good last name to share. His classmate from Yale Law, Trevor McGary, had just been elected U.S. Senator, replacing one of Maine's most-heralded politicians upon her retirement. I had secretly coveted an internship with McGary, but it just wasn't meant to be.

I began looking down at my new license and my registration card. My 2009 Jeep Commander was pushing 200K. Somehow it was still on the road. It was both painted green and burning green. A lot of my peers at Dartmouth had nicer cars than me. I pretended not to care but someday I wondered if I'd drive a crisp SUV or sports car like Jerry Maguire. But for now, I was happy with what I did have. My license was renewed, I had an internship, my Jeep was still running, and I'd be in Bayside all summer. I was feeling confident about my prospects. It was only the Friday before Memorial Day, and there was plenty of time left before we embarked on the dog days of summer.

Memorial Day weekend always brought a promise of something better too. For youngsters like me, it was an opportunity for three months to remake your destiny. Like California to the gold rushers or Plymouth to the Pilgrims, the summer represented a new chance for personal success. Instead of being tied to a library desk spending money, I was tied to a job making money. Though if I am being honest, maybe I enjoyed both. If I met the right people, kept my nose out of trouble, and had the right attitude, my last year in Hanover might not have been so bad. Maybe it didn't matter where I went to law school as long as I passed the LSAT and eventually the bar. Instead of comparing myself to my wealthier classmates, perhaps I would compare myself to my prior outlook.

Dartmouth was a fantastic place to call home for eight months, though it did come with some surprises beyond just the socioeconomic components. I always thought that I was smart in high school, and I guess I was because I got into an Ivy League college, but my friends there were like, *beyond* smart. Family members used to laugh when I would get random questions right once and a while on *Jeopardy!* My dorm neighbors would get every question right it seemed with ease. They would talk about debate teams and robotics competitions at places like Groton and Holderness as if I were supposed to know what that meant or where those places were.

Whether I was as smart as them or not was perhaps not particularly relevant in the short term, because I had come a long way already. Humility and gratitude were a huge part of how I was raised, and it was deeply rooted in where I grew up. A lot of kids I knew growing up would do anything for the opportunities I had, so it was imperative that I didn't forget where I came from.

As I was walking out of the BMV, I looked down at my old driver's license. The sixteen-year-old version of me was nearly unrecognizable. Long swishy hair as opposed to a parted fade. Patchy beard instead of a clean-cut shave. It was like I was trying to cast an actor to play me back then, all wide-eyed the day my father drove me to Rockland just to get this foolish picture taken. I stared at it for a few seconds longer.

"Hey Bakeman, what's up man!" a familiar voice shouted from across the way, breaking my daze. It was a former teammate of mine, Adam Olsen, who I remembered lived down this way somewhere for a bit. I'm pretty sure he went to high school in Camden or Rockland. Most people my age called him AO for short. Adam looked similar to how I last remembered him. His swooshy hairstyle hadn't yet been abandoned, and you could tell that his athletic lifestyle kept him in shape. We played youth hockey together and occasionally he showed up at the men's league games I frequented. Adam ended up going to Chamberlain College and playing varsity hockey there. I suppose we shared an interest in that sport, but also our academic prowess. He was smart as hell too but also the kind of guy who a lot of people could both love and hate simultaneously if they didn't understand his ego.

"Not much, AO. What're you doing here?" I asked.

"My girlfriend works down there at the ice cream stand in Thomaston." He motioned his hand in the direction of the south end of town. "I had to drop off my brother's dog at the vet next door, and now I'm waiting to meet her here."

"You're waiting to meet your brother's dog?"

"No, Billy. I'm meeting my girlfriend here. She's also just got a new car."

"Cool. Cool," I replied, dreading the inevitability of small talk and embarrassed by my slip-up. "What are you up to this summer?" I asked, trying to recover.

"I'm interning with Senator McGary!" he replied with excitement.

This was, of course, the same Senator McGary to whom my uncle knew from law school. It wasn't surprising because Adam was a bright kid who had political interests. He was also the kind of guy who even in middle school had everyone in his back pocket. I didn't know him much in high school though, outside of occasional hockey that is.

McGary was a longtime lawyer and regional businessman who recently defeated an automotive tycoon and former gubernatorial candidate in a very close senate election two years ago. It was strange for two non-politicians to be U.S. Senate nominees, but so goes the times. Pundits from around the country praised the newly-elected McGary for his intellect, though many still considered his victory an electoral upset. Neither surprised me, Adam was made for Washington someday and McGary was ambitious in his own right.

"That's awesome," I said with an internal grimace. "It'll be a great experience."

"For sure. I'll mostly be working out of the Brunswick office. Maybe some trips up to Bangor... We'll see," Adam peered beyond me for a moment.

"Oh look," he continued. "Here comes Megan, I'll introduce you."

I turned around to see who he was talking about. A black Chevy Malibu turned into the driveway and a familiar young woman emerged. It was none other than Megan LaMarre, a former classmate of mine - who I gathered must have been the girlfriend that AO was talking about. Perhaps Adam didn't realize that I already knew Megan. After all, it was a small region and everyone pretty much knew everyone, especially if your high school years overlapped.

Megan LaMarre, of course, was an A-plus certified knockout. She had dark brown hair, a seasonal tan even for May, and plenty else going on if you know what I mean. She went to high school with me for a couple of years but left for our senior year when she transferred to a private school way down in Portland. If I remember correctly, Megan was an only child and her folks now lived in Lincolnville Beach, another town near Bayside and still resting along Penobscot Bay. She was one of those girls, who, after we all graduated, you weren't sure if she was going to end up designing fashion in Boston or married to a local mechanic with two kids already. From what I could tell today, she was more on track with the first path. Megan wore jean shorts, a slimmer fit UMaine tee shirt, and Ray Bans. I couldn't tell what kind of sandals she wore.

Growing up, she had already been a crush, or at least a favorite Instagram account, of most guys my age in the Midcoast. I was no exception to that pattern. We ran in the same circles at Belfast

High, until Megan changed schools just before our senior year began. Before that, we had a short-lived romance during my junior year. My buddies teased that I would someday write her name in big letters on Belfast's water tower. There were also rumors that Megan and I made out behind my friend's car that spring, but I can neither confirm nor deny that.

It was no surprise though that Megan was dating Adam Olsen now, given his smooth persona and innate popularity. I hypothesized that they had met via Tinder over the holiday break when they were both in the area. Possibly she went to school further south near Adam, I frankly had no idea. Chamberlain College was about equidistant between the Midcoast and Portland, and at the endpoint of a major railroad, easily accessible if Megan had been in Boston or other points north of the city. I'd soon find out though, as she quickly recognized me standing next to her boyfriend.

"Oh my word, Billy! So great to see you. How long has it been? Three years?!"

It had only been five months since she and her dad saw me at the Christmas tree farm over in Searsmont back in December. I lied anyway.

"Yeah, probably!"

"What've you been up to?" she asked.

"Well, I'm starting my internship with Bakeman & Courtier in Camden on Tuesday...the law firm. It'll be different not working in Belfast, but I'm alright with it."

"That's neat, with your uncle right? I'm sure Adam told you about his internship too?"

"Yeah, he did."

"Way better than scooping ice cream."

"Definitely," I replied while chuckling, trying not to sound condescending. We then spent the next few minutes shooting the breeze and talking about everything from the warmer weather to the Celtics playoff chances. Turns out she hadn't yet gone to school and was taking classes online for now. Perhaps just another reminder for me to not judge a book by its cover.

"Well, what do you say we get going Meg?" Adam interjected, almost as if he was tired of talking on the sidewalk.

"Oh, right." Megan blushed. "We're going to be in Bayside for a couple of nights! Adam's cousin lives there in the summers and is throwing a party tomorrow night for the long weekend."

Megan gestured toward Adam as if she wanted him to invite me. They both knew I lived there, yet I didn't recall this cousin from any prior conversation.

"Hey, Billy, you should come to the party tomorrow night. A bunch of our old teammates are going to be there and you might even be able to meet some new girls," he said with a smirk.

"Yeah, I should go," I replied, wondering if he was just trying to be nice because he and Megan thought I was a loner. "It'll be good for me to get out, I haven't seen some of the guys in a while."

"Great!" Megan shouted. "I'll text you the address. Still the same number as high school?"

"Yep, same one."

"See you then buddy, 7:30," Adam said as they walked away.

A social life. What a glorious thing to have.

***

My family lived in a modest house on Bluff Road in Northport, a stone's throw from Bayside Village. Its style was that of a colonial, but the third-floor attic was simply filled with keepsakes and storage at this point. Like most of its kind in New England, our home was painted white with dark green shutters. The siding had seen better days, but we had a small front porch, erected in recent years to join our granite steps. Old Glory flew in the doorway, a reminder of what many sacrificed for our privileges.

My parents bought the home in their mid-twenties, right before the turn of the century. Mom, also known as Helen to her friends or Principal Bakeman to her students, was well-liked locally for her work as an educator and community member. She knew everyone, and everyone knew her. She was fearless in her convictions, but still compassionate for others. Mom was the kind of woman who didn't like being taken lightly.

Dad shared a tax office with an old friend of his. It was over on Route 1 in East Belfast. Come spring, all of my friends' parents wanted a chat with Dad, also known as Martin or Marty, about their returns or expected refunds. He often scoffed at my suggestion that there should be a flat tax and was slightly disappointed when I decided to pursue law instead of finance or economics. He and I were fiercely competitive whenever we played board games or were out on the golf course, but it became one-sided whenever trivia was involved. Some folks around here ironically looked down on my parents for having "white collar" jobs, though for the most part, they were well-respected by the citizens they knew. After all, in coastal Maine, the common enemy was more so the seasonal tourists and those bureaucrat types who threatened our way of life. Or so I always heard.

My sister Lori was finishing her freshman year at the University of Maine. She was very smart, like the rest of the family, and was first in her class in high school. Lori got a full ride with tuition to go up to Orono and she decided she wanted to become a marine biologist. We got along well as siblings and she liked a lot of the things I did. In high school, she played basketball and softball and took all the same classes I had. She needed a job this summer too, but had sort of spent the last three weeks hanging out with friends by night and watching *Grey's Anatomy* by day instead. I suppose she was a stickler for cute doctors.

Lori and Mom were outside on the front porch chatting when I drove into the yard. It was about four o'clock and I wondered why my sister wasn't already out on a Friday night. They spotted my old Jeep and recognized me as I turned into the bottom half of the driveway, or as we called it in Maine, the dooryard.

"How'd it go with the BMV?" Mom asked.

"Thirty-five dollars and a new picture," I replied. "Dad home too?"

"Almost, just finishing up a late filer."

"Figures. Hey Lori, I thought you were going out?"

"Not 'til seven," she said. "See any places for hiring?"

"Everywhere," I replied with a chuckle, but Lori didn't appreciate my facetiousness, and instead rolled her eyes. Like I said, we got along well but I was the sarcastic older brother and she was still the sassy younger sister. Sometimes it flipped. It was nature, after all. They returned to chatting as I headed inside our home.

Living at home this summer was comforting, even though many of my friends at Dartmouth spent their summers sprawled out at their family's second or third guest house all alone. Here I had Lori and my mom to make small talk with. I had my dad to go fishing or golfing with. I was fortunate. My roommate's girlfriend at Dartmouth went to some prep boarding school in Connecticut and barely knew her parents. It sounded miserable. As much as I loved being in Hanover during the school year, Maine was where I belonged long-term. Finding a law school relatively nearby would be hard though. The closest place was the flagship state law school in Portland. Admission, as long as I did well on the LSATs, was perhaps a shoo-in for someone with my credentials. And if I went there, I'd get a chance to focus on marine law like I hoped. A lot of my peers had their eyes on Harvard or Yale to no surprise, but that wasn't me. I was still unsure as to if I even wanted to go immediately or not. A stigma existed in the profession for those kindergarten-to-J.D. types who had never actually done real law work. But this summer I'd be here in Waldo and Knox County, doing my thing, and learning from Uncle Jack. Hopefully, that would help. Moreover, I was saving money on food and rent. So yeah, our house in Northport beat Beverly Hills for now.

Dad arrived right on time for dinner as usual and left his briefcase near the door. For a guy born and raised in the sticks, he sure knew how to fit in both at the office and on a moose hunt. He was the kind of guy who handled a crowd full of work boots and one full of Sperrys the same, and I respected that. From the time I was little, my parents raised Lori and me to appreciate the value of the family dinner. It didn't matter that I had become accustomed to takeout pizza in my dorm room watching the Bruins, or that Lori had plans of some sort tonight, we knew that sitting down together with Marty and Helen was important. That night was pretty laid back, only rotisserie chicken and potato salad, though we didn't complain. After Lori was politely excused to head out with friends, I asked my dad if he needed any help over the weekend, understanding that I'd probably be pretty busy after I started at Bakeman & Courtier.

"Need a hand with anything this weekend, Dad?"

"Nah, not really," he replied. "But I am going to head to Union tomorrow to see about a new lawnmower, and I'm thinking I'll skip the place in town this time. If you wanted to go buy some gas tonight that would save me a few minutes in the morning."

"Sure, I can do that. No problem." I loved driving Dad's truck and would never turn down an opportunity. And he knew that. I had my license for five years, about the same time Dad owned that GMC Sierra. Let's just say I got the old Jeep when he upgraded.

But what started as another benign trip to the gas station ended with a conversation that would change the course of my well-calculated summer plans.

Two

Before I went to fuel up, I decided to swing through Bayside Village and see how many summer residents had gotten an early start on their vacation. It was a great barometer for how busy the store or the weekend would be. It was also the place where Megan and Adam would be having their party tomorrow night so it wouldn't hurt to scope it out ahead of time.

Centuries ago, Bayside Village had been a religious summer compound and the home of social activity year-round. Nowadays, it was simply a colony for seasonal residents who frequented the golf club, the beaches, and the higher-end restaurants in Belfast and Camden. Each home in the village was unlike the rest. Many were built in the late 19th Century and stored with them a seemingly timeless feel of awkward charm. I liken it to a baby stuffing their mouth with cake on their birthday. It can be very cute but you can't look for too long. One particular house was pink with baby blue trim as if Gothic revival had been a creation of the Easter bunny. Another was green with brown fences and crimson window shutters. I half-expected a gnome to walk out the front door.

However, as I drove further down Shore Road, the village started to disappear in the rearview and the dwellings became more modern. Large capes with white siding and wooden porches. Wide colonials with bay windows and nautical blue doors. Most had ocean views and smaller guest cottages adjacent to the main home. The driveways featured Volvos with red and white license plates and

Teslas with blue or yellow gradient plates. Bayside proper is where the wealthy folks came to spend their summers. It was the natural byproduct of having a beautiful coastline. My house was just a few miles away yet it was a mere fraction of the real estate cost. People from away wanted to buy a property along the shoreline so badly, they would sometimes pay cash sight unseen. There were rumors that a home had just sold for nearly fifty thousand dollars over asking, and the guy didn't even require an inspection.

Why? City folks loved it here. The perception was that this place was too perfect to even investigate such potential flaws. No hustle. No bustle. And no crime.

A couple of miles later I passed Kelly Cove Beach, a favorite spot of mine. Like many beaches up the coast of Maine, it was rocky instead of sandy, but I appreciated its natural beauty. Each time I came here, I noticed something different whether it be a new piece of driftwood or a new person fishing. Today, the daily low tide and surf were easier to see, as a result of the full moon this weekend.

Dad's truck continued down Shore Road and then met back up with Bluff Road, at another waterfront called Saturday Cove. This place was more heavily trafficked with boats than Kelly Cove, but it was also much closer to consistent vehicle traffic. I turned left toward where I needed to get gasoline.

The closest station was a couple of miles away from where we lived, just near the town office but still right off of U.S. Route 1. Wakefield's Family Grocery it was called. People from all over town and even Lincolnville would stop there on their way to and from Belfast. A few friends of mine had worked there in high school as their first job, selling booze or pizza to locals. Since it was also a grocery store, it became pretty busy with the summer tourists who resided in Bayside. On a Friday night, there was apt to be somebody who would recognize my dad's truck and be disappointed when it was just me perhaps.

As I pulled into the parking lot, it was pretty busy there. Not too surprising for the night before a long weekend. A gentleman with an older Ford pickup was over near the air machine and it caught my attention. It didn't hurt that there was an open space next to him either. I was probably going to have to wait my turn for an open pump.

When I pulled in next to him, I recognized the man as Myles Jackson, a local guy who many people admired. He was an upstanding person and a true pillar of the small business community. Myles owned a boat repair shop and was pretty successful in business. My dad said that some even wanted him to be a selectman or councilman one day because of his sound character. In his spare time, Myles was a substitute teacher and track coach, which suited him well.

A veteran of the Iraq War, Myles served in the Marines and to no surprise had a strong build, innate athleticism, and a commanding presence. Myles was a handsome guy too, with ice-blue eyes and matted auburn hair that had only started to gray. His wife Tracy, a nurse at Waldo General Hospital, was also very attractive, and some around town knew them as almost "the perfect" couple or family, even though I didn't think they had children.

"Hey Mr. Jackson," I spoke out as I rolled my window down. "You in line too?"

“Oh, hi,” he replied. “Sort of, I’m also just killing some time. You’re Marty’s boy, right?”

“Yeah, I’m Billy Bakeman. How’s it going?”

“I’m doing alright, my wife isn't home yet so I figured if we ain’t cooking then I’d order out for us, so I guess here I am.”

“Makes sense,” I replied with a snicker. “What’s on the menu?”

“Only a few Italians.”

“Sounds like a cheap date,” I again replied jokingly, immediately embarrassed about how that could have come across.

“Nah, it’s the best I got. She’s been gone a lot lately, there must be some late shifts over at the hospital. Or so I suppose,” he scoffed, looking past me momentarily and shaking his head before rolling his eyes and fiddling with his truck door.

“Oh, sorry I said anything.” The suspicion in his tone was hard to miss, but I wanted to brush it off and not overstep.

“No worries buddy, but hey, I don’t want to keep you either,” Myles cautioned.

From what I remember, Mr. Jackson was usually willing to talk to anyone, especially at this moment if he was just killing time. I was surprised that he wasn’t more jubilant for a Friday night. Tonight it sounded like he just wanted to get the hell out of Wakefield’s and back to whatever he was doing.

His phone then started vibrating. “I have to take this anyway,” Myles said. “ But tell your folks I said hello.”

“Will do,” I replied, nodding my head and rolling up the window.

Before I knew it Myles Jackson had sped off into the dusk, his demeanor resembling that of preoccupation and restlessness. He wasn't his normal self, even for a brief moment. Usually, he was laughing or cracking jokes. Other times, he opened up about his days serving in the Marines or as a merchant mariner before that, well before he met Tracy and settled in the Belfast area to start his business. My guess was he wasn't much older than forty or forty-five but had already experienced a full life. I hoped I'd get a chance to talk with him again soon. I hadn't experienced too many interactions with Myles since high school when he was a frequent substitute. He was also very good friends with one of my favorite teachers, Steve Hamilton, despite a difference in age of probably twenty years. Mr. Hamilton grew up on the North Shore of Massachusetts but moved to Maine in his thirties and taught at the school over in Lincolnville, alongside my mom. Eventually, they both made their way to our school district and Helen wound up as principal. If anyone knew what was wrong with Myles Jackson, it would be Mr. Hamilton. They were practically like brothers. But as my mom always said, "Let sleeping dogs lay."

Maybe this wasn't the time to intrude.

The next morning, I woke up to the sound of my dad rustling through the downstairs coat closet. I remembered his keys were still in my shorts pocket from the day before, so he must have been looking for them. I hustled downstairs and gave them back to him, apologizing for the oversight. He didn't care much but joked that he knew where I lived if I didn't return them next time.

Eventually, I moseyed my way back upstairs to my bedroom. It was still way messier than I wanted it to be. A tort law textbook from the fall semester was still on top of my bureau. My Tim Thomas poster was cockeyed and there was a pair of boat shoes on the floor blocking the entryway. I'd probably need those tonight at the party, I thought, so I set them next to the camping chair I had in the far corner of the bedroom.

Once I got dressed and returned downstairs to the foyer, I overheard Lori and Mom talking about the news across the house in the living room. The local CBS station was on in the background, and Senator McGary was standing in the hall of the Capitol touting a new bill he was sponsoring to make it easier for citizens of border towns in Maine to buy medicine in Canada. One of the anchors praised him for working so hard when the Senate was about to close again for the holiday weekend.

"What a great idea," Lori said. "Imagine being able to get cheaper pharmacy stuff in Canada rather than pay up the ass here."

"Hey, watch it!" Mom stammered.

"Sorry, it's just interesting..." Lori trailed off only to start up again when I appeared. "Oh, good morning Billy, did you hear about this? Is it legal?"

"I'm not sure, Congress will figure it out I suppose. McGary is a smart guy."

"You should go work for him," my sister suggested.

I gave her a blank stare. There were three outcomes. Either she was completely oblivious to the fact that I already had a job with Uncle Jack, knew that I had one and didn't remember, or thought I should just walk out on a generous family member two days before I was supposed to start interning there. Plus, being an intern in the

Senate didn't just happen overnight. *Oh, wait, unless you're a kiss-ass like Adam Olsen,* I thought.

"No, Lori. I already have a job," I replied, shaking my head. "AO is working for McGary though."

"AO, as in Adam Olsen, like, from hockey?

"Yeah, he has already started there. Probably gonna be rotating between some different state offices."

"That's neat," Mom interjected. "I don't remember him though."

"He's dating Megan LaMarre now, I guess."

"Is that the girl you almost went to Prom with?"

They both asked me that at the same time, emphasizing the word *almost,* but they already knew the answer. This conversation was going nowhere, fast. Lori knew everything, and Mom put it on that she didn't, but as a principal, everyone knew she did. Funny how only one of them remembered AO but they both remembered Megan.

"Yeah, it is. Then she went to some all-girls school in Portland I think."

"Cool. She's pretty," Lori said.

Again, this conversation was going nowhere and I certainly regretted bringing it up. They could tell and freed me to the kitchen to make my breakfast. As I was pouring OJ, I could still hear them talking about Megan, specifically debating the color of her dress at my prom four years ago. *Time to get a job, Lori.* I thought.

As the day went on and on, I expected to get some sort of text from Megan about the party's address. It was probably my imagination, but I think she wanted to catch up and chat longer than we had yesterday. After all, I had changed since high school. Going to school far away from home made me more independent. An old buddy of mine from high school, Hank, who went to a small college not far from Dartmouth, met me in Hanover for a beer or two back before Christmas now that we were both twenty-one. He had noticed a change in me then too. He said I was more laid back. We'll see if that lasts.

Around 3 o'clock, Megan texted me. I wasn't too concerned about getting the address since I probably lived closer than she expected, but that didn't matter since the text was not about the party's location.

Hey Billy. No party tonite. Adam's aunt is coming home early and claiming the house back. Me and him are going to a movie instead. Sorry. Catch up later.

Megan apparently wanted to catch up, but alas it would have to wait. I wasn't too sad about not seeing her again so soon, or AO really for that matter. We had all summer and I guess I had other friends too. That said, I still pondered that the Saturday of a long weekend was both a great time to catch up with people I hadn't seen in a while and a good time to relax. Most likely I would be doing the latter. I know Lori had plans again tonight, so I imagined she was going to go to the same movie they were.

The cinema in Belfast, if you could even call it that, was a small three-screen theater from the early 1900's. It had bright neon red lettering across the front, with its name, *The Colonial,* in sort of a pre-war Hollywood font. There was a huge ass elephant on the roof, for whatever reason I don't know. The front of the building was two shades of green mixed with some random shades of purple and crimson for trim. Much like everything else in Belfast, the theater was quirky, quaint, and charming. It was both literally and figuratively a pillar of the community. The theater was saved once from extinction but some believed the movies were still a dying breed. I hoped not. That place had memories.

For me tonight though, the theatre wasn't the choice. Odds were my sister, her friends, and Adam and Megan would be there already so going alone or asking other friends this late felt contrived and lame. My new plan was to simply stay home with my parents, watch the Red Sox, and maybe drop a fishing line in the river before dusk. A far cry from a Saturday night on the Dartmouth campus, but fine by me. Though for what may have seemed like the second quiet evening in as many days would once again alter the course of my well-calculated plans.

***

The third inning had come and gone, and the Sox were winning 6-0 after a couple big hits. For a team that had won so much in my lifetime already, they still felt incredibly inconsistent so half of me wanted to wait and see if they finished the job. But, of course, I am who I am so naturally the other half was getting restless and couldn't stop thinking about two things. The first was why Myles was so paranoid last night and the second was that I could use some time fishing.

It was only a little before seven-thirty, with at least an hour left before it was completely dark. My parents were half asleep already, and it didn't take that much racket to retrieve my fishing gear from the downstairs closet. Within a couple of minutes, I was already driving down toward a small river that eventually fed into Kelly Cove and Penobscot Bay.

I parked along the side of the road and shuffled down to the water. The air was cool and salty. My sneakers slid a little in the mud. Crickets and frogs set the soundtrack for the next few minutes, with the occasional car driving down the road. A few hundred feet away from the trail to the river, there was a yellow sign that cautioned drivers to slow down ahead of the curve. Not many did, and I didn't blame them. Nevertheless, they had to twist and turn fast to correct which of course caused the noises. My Jeep probably startled them too, especially if their headlights weren't on yet.

My red and white fishing bobber had sat quietly for a few minutes now. No action whatsoever since I had baited the hook and sunk the line. There was a neat reflection in the water, as the twilight bounced off the ripples. The darkening sky changed the complexion of the red on the bobber, and time seemed to stand still as I hunched on the horizontal log near the river.

It wasn't uncommon to come across brook trout in the river, even if the pond or stream hadn't been stocked in the spring. Some Atlantic salmon even used these brooks to spawn after their journey to sea. I didn't expect to be that lucky though.

Fishing always brought out the calmness I craved, in a different way than other sports or activities could. Each passing moment was an appreciation for the environment around me and how it came to be, combined with an equally significant focus on the here and now. If I spent too much time daydreaming, I could lose a bite. But if I worried too frequently about the trivial catch I might reel in, I would miss the forest for the trees. Literally.

A few more minutes passed and I began to see the line sink and hop, along with the multicolored sphere that hovered on the water. My hands moved quickly to reel in what probably was nothing more than a sunfish when suddenly I heard a loud engine behind me break my focus.

I turned around quickly and saw a larger, SUV-style vehicle barreling past the trailhead up by the road, but I couldn't see much else through the trees and incline. A couple more seconds elapsed when I heard a second loud noise.

CLANG.

It sounded like metal on metal. My interest in catching a fish that evening was soon replaced by a curiosity as to what the hell had just happened on the road. The sunfish was long gone. I grabbed my bait, pole, and tackle box and whisked my way through the ferns and bushes back up to the end of the trail.

When I reached the road again, I looked to my left and saw nothing. Then, I whirled my head around to the right and saw tire marks scuffed along the pavement. I followed them down the road. The breeze was either cooler than I had remembered or I had a shiver up my back. It wasn't often that I got spooked, but I couldn't yet figure out where the noise came from. Surely there wasn't a car off the road, that would have been louder. Danger usually avoided me. Heck, I was the kid who never broke any bones despite playing hockey. I tried not to worry.

As I got closer to the yellow caution sign, I noticed it was bent pretty badly. The steel post was at an obtuse angle and the yellow paint itself had been scraped. A mix of blue or black paint and black scuffs had replaced some of the mustard yellow paint on the sign. Daylight was becoming a problem, so I slid out my cell phone and used it as a flashlight. It was possible that a car had swerved to avoid my parked Jeep, lost control, and hit the sign. Yet it was kind of miraculous that the driver hadn't gone off the road.

On my way back to the Jeep, I knelt to pick up my fishing gear that had been left in the ditch. My head was spinning again, trying to figure out if I knew someone who lived around here who could be in danger. It was pretty dark now, so while I packed up my things, I used the open hatchback of the Jeep as a light source.

Out of the corner of my eye, I saw another pair of headlights. This time, the vehicle was moving slower. Their lights illuminated me from a distance, but I didn't catch much else through the glare or the space between us. Once the driver saw me, they pulled a U-turn before I could see anything more. This road did eventually loop back around, though it didn't make much sense for someone to come from the south twice, presuming it was the same driver who hit the sign unless they were trying to get to the cove. It was probably just a drunken driver who thought maybe I noticed the sign and would tell someone. It was so dark that I couldn't just assume it was the same vehicle though anyway.

The truth always comes out in the light, I thought. Much like the night before, everything seemed benign. However, at the same time, I still had this aching feeling that something wasn't quite right in my sleepy town.

Three

Mourning doves were my wake-up call the next morning, though I am quite sure that sleep wasn't on the menu last night anyway. My mind was still pacing about what had happened at the brook. *Who was that driver? Why did he turn around?* Something didn't add up. The added ambiguity of Myles' actions on Friday also kept entering my mind. Perhaps it was the result of not seeing the guy in a year or two. Maybe he was just different now. A post-pandemic economy hurt a lot of small businesses around here. His might not be different. I can't imagine it was easy to run a business like his these days with everyone, including him, probably strapped for cash.

And, it was a holiday weekend. Who is to say that the driver wasn't just a flatty who was lost or drunk or both? Hard to imagine someone just stumbling upon Bayside though unless they were going somewhere on purpose. The high school kids liked to go for joy rides these days too, probably bored of driving to the now non-existent Bangor Mall or something like that. One of them likely thought I would squeal on the busted road sign.

Sunday mornings were usually spent getting ready to head into town for church, but today Dad and Uncle Jack were preparing to host the tri-annual Bakeman family cookout. It typically occurs three times a year around the three major "summer holidays." Dad's younger sister Nora would be there too with her husband Scott. They lived in Stockton Springs, further up the bay. Last Labor Day the party was at our house so this year it would be down in Camden at Jack's place. His house was nicer than ours, but no one cared to mention it. He and my aunt Bonny had been married a long time, sweethearts from college I guess. They had a swimming pool and a stone patio, so I think everyone looked forward to going there this afternoon. It was supposed to be pretty hot for this time of year.

Mom and Dad were bringing steaks and another potato salad. Jack was cooking hot dogs to go with the steaks and I guessed that Aunt Nora would bring booze of some kind with another side dish. I suspected Nora's kids would come too, my cousins. They were eight and six. I didn't have much in common with them of course.

Jack and Bonny didn't have any kids, and as a result, I expected Jack to talk to me when he wasn't grilling. Being thankful for the internship opportunity he gave me was an understatement. But at the same time, I didn't want to be a kiss ass yet I certainly wanted to make him and my dad proud. There would likely be a few family friends that stopped by too, so I'd have an opportunity to talk to others as well. When we arrived, Jack greeted us at the front steps holding a red Budweiser bottle in his left hand and his outstretched arm for a handshake in his other. It was eleven-thirty.

"Hey buddy, hey Lori! Welcome!"

My sister leaned in for a hug and I shook his hand.

"Hey Uncle Jack, good to see you," I said. My parents trailed behind, and Dad cheerfully slapped him on the back upon the greeting.

"Last time I'll see you before I'm your boss," Jack said with a laugh. I chuckled and nodded.

"He won't give you any trouble!" my Dad interjected with an equally as big Bakeman-style laugh.

"Wouldn't be surprised if that's true, Marty. Honors this term again! That's impressive even for a Dartmouth student. I read the paper."

Of course, a Yalie would say that. I laughed with them again before we stepped inside. The cast of characters was as I predicted. Aunt Bonny was over in the corner, stirring a punch bowl and wearing a navy sundress. She then retreated to the back of the kitchen and pulled a wine bottle out of a thin bag made from recycled sails. *I guess we're starting early.*

Pretty soon I saw Uncle Scott, a tough Army guy who was more interested in whatever game was going to be on TV than this gathering. His kids jumped around the patio blowing bubbles from some of those little jars. It warmed my heart that kids still knew how to do that. Aunt Nora emerged from behind the screen door, her sunglasses tumbling to the floor. She picked them up and then hugged me, asking about school and what courses I liked and disliked from junior year.

When she moved on to the kitchen, I found my way to the lawn where I sat down and sipped on a glass of the punch Bonny stirred. There was a slight taste of rum in there, so I took it quicker than usual. A few more familiar faces emerged, like friends whom Dad, Jack, and Aunt Lori knew from school, old neighbors, and such. One of them was there with their son, who was a couple of years younger than me. If he saw me, he'd want to talk about his frat life at UMaine, so I stayed clear of that to avoid any awkward conversations with my sister still in earshot.

Then I saw Tom Milton, the chief of Police in Belfast. He and the Bakemans had been friends since their shared adolescence. His mother and my grandma knitted together. My dad and uncle played football with him at Belfast High back in the glory days. He was tall, muscular, and had short blonde hair. His amber eyes were hidden behind the blue lenses of a new pair of Oakleys. For a police chief, Tom wasn't intimidating at all, to the surprise of most. He was so personable, and rooted in his Christian faith, that people often told him he should be a radio host or a clergyman. Like my father and uncle, Chief Milton, sometimes called Major Tom as a joke, was in his late forties. While they all had different professions that sometimes intersected, the three remained close friends through their adult lives. And of course, as a family friend, he had watched me grow up and therefore recognized me as I sat down in an Adirondack chair.

The gathering was still centered at the front of the patio near the pool, so it was just us on the periphery of the lawn. Tom started to walk over toward me, holding a can of Pepsi in one hand and his iPhone in the other.

"Billy! How's it going?" he said, setting his soda down on the chair.

"I'm well, Tom – I mean, uh Chief, how about yourself?"

"Doing well, happy to stop by today. Haven't seen you or your sister in forever."

Tom was right. It had been a couple of years with school and everything. He hadn't been at last year's cookouts. Tom's son was a freshman when I was a senior, so we only played sports together for one year. Pretty soon he and I were chatting about my internship, the weather forecast, and what we thought of this year's Patriots draft picks, including the new quarterback. He probably felt a little bit out of place at the Bakeman gathering, even though he was a family friend, however, you couldn't tell. We then joined the rest of the group and everyone started sharing stories that had happened since the last time we all saw one another.

Soon after, the group conversation dissipated and everyone split off again while Jack was grilling. My sister and Aunt Bonny were sharing the newest celebrity gossip with Mom. Meanwhile, Nora was trying to entertain her kids while Scott and my dad shared theories about fishing. Some of the neighbors recognized Chief Milton and decided to go play with the kids instead of talking to a cop, which I guess I understood. I started to join in with Dad and Uncle Scott, sort of unsure as to which conversation to bite at first. Then I noticed Tom take a phone call and drift back toward the house. His face grew serious and he didn't say much. Deciding this was a great time to "use the bathroom," and eavesdrop on what might be happening, I discreetly followed him.

When I got inside, I purposefully used the bathroom upstairs closest to the window that he was standing under outside, positioning myself so I didn't make any noise and kneeling so I couldn't be seen. At that moment, Tom wasn't speaking, but rather just murmuring whatever information he was being told. Then, he finally spoke, uttering words that immediately got my attention.

"Thanks for getting everyone involved so fast Sara," he said. "Do you think there's an ongoing threat?"

I couldn't make out her response. I guessed that Tom was speaking with Sara Lopez, a Sheriff's deputy in Waldo County. She was the main deputy for Northport within the County Sheriff's Office and most locals knew her from back when she was a high school basketball standout. If something was going down in our neck of the woods, Lopez was usually the first one there. Whatever happened was probably just outside of Tom's immediate jurisdiction, but very freaking close to my house. Deputy Lopez seemed to be giving him a personal call since he wasn't near his scanner.

"Well that's just bullshit," Major Tom replied quickly. "There's no way he runs off on that gal. When I get back to the station, have them share a copy of Tracy's – the wife's – statement with me."

Deputy Lopez continued talking, but I couldn't help but wonder if a domestic dispute or something was going on here.

"The main thing is, we want to be notified here and work in concert. Jackson knows a lot of people in town so we may be able to leverage that to find him."

I froze. Jackson. Tracy.

Chief Milton had to be talking about Myles and Tracy Jackson. It had been less than forty-eight hours since I saw Myles at the gas station and I knew something was up then. But Tom was right, Myles wouldn't run off on his wife if that was the going theory for whatever was happening.

"Thanks again for keeping us in the loop. I'm at a party but I'll leave now and talk to my guys on duty. Take care, Sara." Tom looked back down at his iPhone and peered up the driveway, walking toward his car as I peeked through the window.

I'm horrible at lip reading, but make no mistake I knew what he was saying to whoever was on the phone now.

"We have a missing persons case."

***

By the end of the party, folks had figured out that Tom must've left for a work-related reason, as most knew it was unlike him to leave so abruptly. I did not share what I had heard with anyone because I did not want to admit I was eavesdropping. Instead, I played dumb like the rest of them and went merrily along eating the steaks, chicken, and whatever else my family had cooked up. With each additional hour that went by, the episode with Tom started to vanish from my recent memory, only to creep back in every time a car went by in the distance. If I showed any sense of alarmism, I'd perhaps expose myself as being preoccupied with anything other than what normal college kids like me were supposed to worry about.

A struggle throughout my life to date was that I took things too seriously. While not a clinical psychologist by any means, my recent hypothesis was that I did so in hopes of being taken seriously myself. My biggest fear - beyond of course the loss of life and things of that nature - was that I would ultimately underachieve in my later years and never amount to anything substantial. I was Ivy League smart, but not Ivy League rich. I was strong in my internal convictions but often failed to communicate them effectively. I wasn't a loser, but I also didn't have a lot of friends. I was athletic, but not that good at sports. While adults would call it, "being well-rounded," I was afraid it was just a euphemism for being mediocre. *A jack of all trades but a master of none.* Home videos taken by my father would recall me once exclaiming at the age of four that everyone thought I was stupid. So I over-compensated as a teen and now as a young adult and took everything too seriously.

Whether this was and is accurate or not in the big picture, I guess time will tell. But it is hard to deny that this state of mind led me to what I felt at the moment. Myles Jackson was missing. I had seen him days before in a preoccupied state of his own. To me, there's no way that was a coincidence. And if there was something to be done to help, I was damned well going to try.

When we got home, Mom did some work and Dad fiddled with the new lawn mower outside. Lori stayed in her room and watched TikTok videos, much to the chagrin of the rest of us. The Red Sox had already played a game this afternoon, wearing their camouflage jerseys, and beat Milwaukee rather-handedly. There was no game to watch until the Celtics tipped off tonight at nine for the third game of the conference finals. I thought about just watching Netflix or something, considering it was a family tradition to go to a Memorial Day parade in the morning and I'd have to wake up pretty early.

While my computer powered up, I sat on my bed and scrolled through Instagram for a couple of minutes. I stumbled across a recent photo of Megan and Adam, who appeared to spend all afternoon at a party similar to the one I was at. My finger hovered over the "like" button, but I decided to click on Adam's profile instead. It had the usual suspects in his bio, his hockey team name and number, a few emojis, and his class year. It also had a tag linking it to Megan's profile next to a heart. It was so juvenile of me to be doing this, but I clicked on it anyway, going straight over to Megan's profile.

Her first picture was of her childhood dog, very typical. The next was with Adam at Faneuil Hall from what looked like last weekend. Then the third photo was of her mom for Mother's Day.

After that there was a photo of her new car, a blue Ford Bronco. I had seen her driving a Chevy sedan on Friday, but that could have been her old car, so maybe something was going on that also involved a trip to the BMV that day. Perhaps her family was getting ready to sell it or something. I frankly had no idea and didn't care that much. It seemed like a lot of minutiae for me to ponder, taking away from what was a great picture of the car, and also, a great picture of Megan.

There was some history between us in high school, but I didn't feel that way about her anymore. At least not right now. If asked, I would always admit that she was attractive and of course, I would always be slightly jealous of Adam based on the history he and I had anyway, though I was just satisfying my innate curiosity. The truth of the matter was, that these people wanted to be my friends and I was trying to judge people less. So far that was still a work in progress.

In the photo, Megan leaned up against the side of the Bronco, holding a set of keys, and her other hand displayed a thumbs-up sign. She wore a pair of Nike gym shorts, and a red tee shirt, and had a Sea Dogs hat on her head. I chuckled a little, before swiping left to see a similar picture of her when I knew her best, more than likely an inspiration for the one I had just seen. In that installment, she was a few years younger and standing at the Chevy dealership over by the old Wendy's in town, perching in front of the same older black Malibu I had seen on Friday. In many ways, Megan was exemplifying the coming of age that most expected out of adolescent teens. Going from a smaller car to a bigger one, from the country to the city, from one job to the next. She had talked about working retail during the holidays when we saw her in Searsmont last Christmas. I had no doubt she worked hard for what she got now despite her family's vast wealth, and I genuinely felt happy for her. Even Adam, who I had once seen as a rival, still probably deserved his internship with McGary, even though he could be a little bit of a freeloader at times.

Like any young adult, I balanced the dos and don'ts of social media as well as an ant would balance a bowling ball, so before I accidentally liked an image of Megan's from two years ago, I quickly exited her profile and began my Netflix show, wondering if it was even still worth it or if I should go watch *60 Minutes* with my dad. Before long again though, I fell back into the trap of going on my phone, this time opening Facebook and seeing something that immediately got my attention.

My high school classmate's mother had just shared a post from Tracy Jackson, which made sense since they were both nurses and probably knew one another professionally. In the post, Tracy asked if anyone had seen Myles today, explaining that she had already called the police after he didn't come home on Saturday. This corroborated what I had heard from Chief Milton earlier today, and set my mind into a frenzy again. Myles could have told Tracy on Friday night that he saw me at the gas station, which would almost certainly lead police to question me since they would eventually exhaust all sources of information. If I told them he acted differently than normal, what would their conclusion be? Would it help or hurt my situation and his? Surely if Milton knew more about Tracy's statement than he did at the time, he would have approached me at the party. Or maybe she didn't mention me at all because Myles didn't either. If I contacted the police and told them of my concern ahead of time, I risked exposing myself as an idiot and even worse, increased the risk that I would be seen as Belfast's version of Richard Jewell.

Then there was Saturday night. The mysterious and enigmatic driver near the fishing hole was the second peculiar experience in as many nights. And for a town and region so dedicated to maintaining an image of placidity, both felt out of place to me. A series of events unfolded which at first could have been separate from one another. Myles could just have been grumpy about his dinner options. This driver could have simply been lost or drunk. Chief Milton could have been working on any old domestic case. But now I at least knew that the first and the third events were connected based on Myles as the common denominator. His different attitude was a sign of distress for a man who was usually joyful. Perhaps he planned to do something dangerous, or maybe he was the one in danger. The one hole in my weekend timeline was the event in the middle. My concern for my safety was heightened, but in my mind, the only way to quell it was to return to the scene. I had to go find out more about what happened last night on Shore Road, but I needed to do it alone.

Dad was on the couch, watching Anderson Cooper draw on about some current event, who knows what. Something about insider trading, I thought I heard. I told Dad I'd be back in a couple hours, and that I was going to watch the Celtics at Gillie's with a few friends. I hated lying but I needed to do this without someone worrying about me or connecting the dots. The truth is, he probably doubted I would spend that much time at Gillie's anyway. It was Belfast's version of a sports bar, but we never actually sat at the bar. There was usually a high top in the corner that we staked out, with a good view of the game. Near the window, there was a rounded booth where a lot of my former teachers would spend their Friday evenings. Gillie's was a wholesome spot if I was being honest about something, but the fine establishment was not my destination right now.

Within a few minutes, I arrived at the brook and parked in the same spot at first. Knowing it could get dark quick, I retrieved a flashlight from my Jeep's storage console. I walked briefly around and surveyed the culverts for signs that someone had consumed too much alcohol, but there were no signs of freshly disposed bottles or cans that I hadn't already seen yesterday. Moving on, I began walking on the road in the direction of the beach at Kelly Cove where I knew the brook came out, wondering if whoever this was who wanted to avoid me could have initially parked there to get their drinking fix.

People enjoyed hanging out at this cove because it was so remote and peaceful. You only knew about it if you frequented Bayside or if you happened to be driving on this end of Shore Road, usually heading to and from the village. But there was nobody here tonight. In the distance, I heard the sound of waves, with an occasional stirring coming from one of the nearby residences, most likely some vacationers here for the long weekend. The air was chillier than I expected, considering how warm it was at the party today. There wasn't anything of value on the ground here either, which made me question what the hell I was even trying to accomplish. Tying this area and that vehicle to Myles' disappearance felt like a stretch with each moment that passed by.

I trekked further down the beach and noticed some Heineken cans stacked on one another close to the rocks. One was still half-full, and it hadn't rained in days. Littering like that was unusual for an area that was so exclusive, so I began to ease a little bit. The sun was still up for now, and the twilight cast a glare on the cove, illuminating the far corner where the brook came out. To satisfy my ultimate curiosity, which was already now waning as a result of the beer cans, I decided to circle back to my Jeep via the brook. I had fished there many times, including last night, and knew that even at dusk there would be enough light to navigate back to the main road and go home.

When I reached the treeline, I had to be careful not to trespass, as there was one house I knew was close to the water. My watch vibrated, telling me I had reached my step goal for the day, which was sad since it took until just past eight o'clock to do so. With each step, I carefully adhered to the small path along the brook, approaching a small area where I knew it got swampy before continuing back toward the road. There wasn't a plan here, mostly just a sense of uncharacteristic risk on my behalf. This place was probably full of ticks. When I was in Boy Scouts, I had once ended up with seven ticks on my body during one hike. I wouldn't doubt if this trek rivaled that experience, but so far it had both eased my paranoia and brought me back to my adventurous side again, which wasn't truly present when I was at Dartmouth. Not many kids from Westchester wanted to jaunt through the woods at night with no real strategy.

Suddenly, I noticed a random shoe on the ground from behind a rock, close to the swamp and deep in the grass. Miraculously, I didn't trip on it as it wasn't that far away from the path. Daylight was becoming an issue again, so I tried to kick it out of the way, only to soon realize it was attached to someone's leg further in the grass. My body immediately ached, including my heart as it exploded to beat at a rapid rate.

The pants rolled up as I kicked at the leg, the remaining daylight exposing a leg tattoo that read:

SEMPER FI

2002-2009

JACKSON

My mental consciousness must have dipped in and out over the next couple of minutes, but one thing I said I remembered.

"Holy shit, this is Myles Jackson."

Four

"We've got trouble in Bayside," I remember Deputy Lopez reporting over her radio. "Calling for backup and state. There's a body at Kelly Cove. We need to seal the area."

She was standing next to me, and I was leaning up against a tree, dazed.

Thank you, Jesus, I thought. For a moment and through my shock I wondered if I had even called the police yet. I would later learn that Lopez was in the area already, on her way back home, and took my call via the 911 dispatcher. She came to the scene from the road, where my Jeep was, and hadn't done much of anything else until this moment. A state trooper had been patrolling traffic on Route 1 and helped coordinate with the Sheriff's Office to close the perimeter and start the investigation.

My mind was still dazed. I wondered what the next steps would be in my own life. They weren't going to let me walk away without taking my statement. Would I have to explain my suspicion or would a less complicated version of the truth be sufficient? Pretty soon, I was led back to the road, where I sat on the bumper of my Jeep while the Statie prepared to take my statement. He was a tall man, probably six-five, and he wore a trooper cap that made him look like a cross between Andy Griffith and a Telly Savalas character.

In many ways, I was scared to tell them the truth about why I was there. I was alone. There was no fishing gear with me and no beach items. To them it could look like I was here for a reason, maybe even to dispose of Myles Jackson. Billy Bakeman was not a liar, though, and certainly not one to a police officer, so I decided to tell them the simplest facts without getting in the weeds: I was here because I had seen someone hit a sign the night before and wondered if it was a drunk driver who had destroyed any other property. I even showed him the yellow sign and explained the part about the SUV turning around. My soon-to-be-lawyer instinct kicked in I suppose.

He then asked if I knew anything about the body and I explained that I thought it could be Myles Jackson, describing the ankle tattoo. He clearly had thought of that conclusion already but didn't say so. Instead, he nodded. My voice shook as I broke down the sequence of events leading to the discovery minutes prior. And when he asked if I had seen Jackson recently, I told them in passing at Wakefield's Grocery on Friday. The officer then explained to me that it appeared "the victim" had been in a fight, was badly beaten, and had even been shot as well.

"So you think you saw this guy on Friday and then you came out here looking for beer cans and an SUV only to discover this body?"

"Yes," I replied. "It's awful."

"And you didn't touch the body once you found it?"

"No, sir. I just tripped on the leg." I assured him.

"And this vehicle you mentioned, do you know anything else about it?"

"Just that it hit that sign and then came back," I said, motioning over toward the side of the road. "I thought they might come back tonight."

I regretted saying that last part almost immediately.

"Okay, son, we'll take it from here with the detective work. You're a primary witness in this situation, but right now you're not a suspect here. Just do as we say and ask and you shouldn't have any problems," he said. "I'm gonna have a detective come by your house tomorrow morning to start that side of things. Go call your folks."

"Can I drive home now?"

"I'll have Lopez escort you. I understand it's only a mile or two."

This probably goes without saying, but my mother was the first to the door when Lopez arrived with me. The idea of an officer accompanying her son to the door was not something that she had on her bingo board this morning. I thought this was all kind of unnecessary, even given the circumstances. I was almost twenty-two years old for crying out loud. My parents didn't have legal authority over me, but they did however own the home.

Helen was immediately concerned upon opening the door but her mood changed just as fast when Lopez explained what was going on tonight. Facebook was a common site for my mom too, and she soon realized the situation to which Lopez was referring. Obviously, with an ongoing investigation, details were not shared, but Mom was joined by Dad at the door when Lopez told them a detective would be visiting in the morning. It was mostly a blur to me. By the end of the conversation, Mom and Dad knew that I had come across a dead body and that I would be questioned further by a detective who was leading the case. And because they're smart, I'm sure they put it together that this person was Myles Jackson.

When the deputy left, Dad looked me square in the eye.

"I didn't know Kelly Cove was on the way to Gillie's from here, and I've lived in this home twenty-seven years."

I paused, then took a breath before speaking. He interrupted me.

"Look, Billy, I'm not as mad at you for lying as much as I am confused as to how you ended up in the woods at Kelly Cove next to a dead body specifically. I know you go fishing over there but what the hell."

"I'm disappointed that you didn't tell us where you were going," Mom said. "You're a man now, you can make your own choices, but you don't have to lie to your father."

"I understand," I replied. "Really...I do." I took a breath before continuing. "Last night I saw a suspicious car. Don't know what it was or where it was going. I thought it might have to do with Myles somehow. Tom left the party because of it all and the timing was weird so I went back there..."

"Spying on a police chief and then going to the woods to look for clues is what that sounds like," Mom said quietly.

"Well, when you say it like that..." I replied.

"And...what am I gonna tell my brother?" Dad asked. "That you can't go to work Tuesday because a detective is coming by?"

"He's coming tomorrow," my mother corrected.

"Doesn't matter. Billy, this is bad shit. I know you did nothing wrong legally but you know what this looks like? It looks like Bakemans screwing around and messing with delicate situations. Your mother is the principal for goodness sake."

After a few minutes, Dad calmed down. I knew he was worried about me, and it came out as frustration, but I didn't blame him. I shouldn't have gone to Kelly Cove tonight, there was no logical explanation for the sequence of events. He and I talked it out and came up with a plan to ease Uncle Jack's reaction. We would frame it like I was just fishing down there and that I called the police immediately. Nothing about eavesdropping on Chief Milton or the paranoia surrounding the SUV that wasn't relevant. That stuff would be in the police report but as long as Jack didn't know, it wouldn't be a problem. Dad and I also determined that the detective would hear the whole truth regardless of whether or not it made me sound crazy. When we were done talking, he patted me on the back.

"It's gonna be okay, son," he said, as he muted the game, the basketball hype-music fading. "Your mom and I are here for you even when you're an adult who gets into trouble."

***

My family departed the next morning for the Memorial Day parade, but I stayed back at the house, sitting on the porch and waiting for the detective to arrive. At times, this felt like a movie. I expected this guy to drive a black Suburban and roll up to our driveway with butlers or something. But then I remembered this was Waldo County. Even Bayside wouldn't demand that kind of fanfare from law enforcement. Though who the hell knew after last night?

After a few minutes of waiting there, I started back into the house to grab a drink when I felt my phone vibrate, it was Adam.

Hey Billy. Sorry again about Saturday. There's another get-together Wednesday if you wanna come?

I decided to text him later. Thursday was my dad's birthday so I could always get creative with the calendar and make that an excuse if I wanted to bail. I'm sure it would just involve some random Chamberlain friends and a few people I knew from Camden or Belfast High, which sometimes could get interesting. Our high schools, and the students within them, had an interesting relationship with one another. We used to be bitter rivals in sports. When I was in high school, for example, their football team beat ours in the regular season to decide home-field advantage in the playoffs and practically had a weeklong celebration, only for our team to go there a couple of days later and obliterate them, winning 50-0 to end their season. Then, on the other hand, our baseball team was routinely eliminated by them in the playoffs, tipping the rivalry back and forth as time passed. It created an awkward relationship when we would play on travel or club teams together in the offseason, as was the case with hockey among others. In Bayside we had the choice to go to either high school, but we still almost always went to Belfast. Despite that, Camden High eventually got so big that they rarely played Belfast in sports anymore because we were too small.

In many ways, it was like a big brother and a little brother bonding over time. Belfast was never going to be Camden, but it didn't need to be. One school had the prettiest auditorium, the windmill, and the expansive cafeteria. The other was only recently renovated. One town was known for its movie-scene backdrop. The other was still in the infancy of its tourism revitalization. Living in Bayside, we were often caught in between. If you talked to some folks, the differences between the two were noticeable and important to point out, while others understood the old money that still influenced

Camden, but shook it off as a superficial characteristic and an inapplicable comparison. Probably by now, neither town gave in too much to the prior way of thinking, even if some held on to decades-old jealousy.

The rekindled friendship between AO and I was an example that young people didn't necessarily adhere to the same regional stereotypes. As adults, maybe we'd work side-by-side together one day and share stories of how we played on the same club team rather than how our schools clashed as youngsters. It was a modest proposal for the future, I suppose, but it wasn't a situation that I cared a lot about right now. The two-minute reminder vibration shuddered on the porch table, but I still ignored the text.

***

Around nine-thirty, the detective arrived. He drove a lifted Dodge Ram with a gray exterior and tinted windows. The vehicle resembled my dad's truck in that it didn't look old, but you knew it had a history. After backing into the driveway, the detective emerged, carrying a notebook and his badge.

In some respects, it was not as you would imagine in films. This man wore black jeans and a light blue shirt. His hair was patchy gray but he still appeared middle-aged. He looked to be about 50. The detective introduced himself as Roger Atkinson, a lead investigator with the State's major crimes unit. Because of the ambiguity around the case, they would be handling the homicide investigation from here on out. At a quick count, this was the fourth different law enforcement officer I had interacted with in twenty-four hours. My career choice was seeming more fitting by the second, and these wouldn't be the last I encountered. However, Atkinson was different. He commanded a sense of seriousness that the others carried but in a less intense manner. Rather, he seemed calm and calculated, something I estimated was the reason for his specific role in the force.

Atkinson began by laying out why I was being questioned but was clear that this was not an interrogation and that he or I could leave at any time if we chose to. He later explained that because of the holiday and the fact that law enforcement didn't want the public jumping to conclusions, they decided to conduct the interview here at my parent's house. I suppose my folks had received this message last night when Lopez had come to escort me home, but I was too distraught to comprehend the situation. Lastly, Atkinson emphasized the importance of transparency in this interview, implying that while I was not a suspect in the disappearance of Myles nor his apparent killing, I could find myself in further danger from the perpetrators if I held back information. I nodded along, and soon the questions began. Atkinson started his recording device.

"State your name please, son."

"Billy Bakeman."

"Your full name."

"William Robert Bakeman," I corrected.

"What is your status as a citizen of Northport and Waldo County?"

"I am a matriculated college student."

"And your whereabouts on Sunday the 26th of May were in Northport, Maine?"

"Yes."

"Were you at the residence of your parents, Martin and Helen Bakeman, around eight o'clock the evening of May 26th?"

"No," I replied. This was beginning to sound like a witness testimony that I'd see on television shows. I half expected Atticus Finch to appear in the corner of our kitchen. The detective continued.

"Were you visiting the area of Kelly Cove on the evening of May 26th?

"Yes," I replied again. So far it seemed like he was just gathering information that he already knew.

"And while at Kelly Cove, you discovered the body of the victim?

"Yes, sir."

"And your visit to Kelly Cove, in Northport, was the nature of it related to the public disappearance of Myles Jackson?"

Understanding the weight of this particular question, I explained my suspicion about the vehicle the night before, wondering if further property damage had been done. I also explained that I had read about Myles' disappearance on Facebook, which gave me an intellectual alibi for eavesdropping on Chief Milton at the cookout. And wondering if the two situations were connected, I walked back to the beach and the brook to see if my suspicions were true.

Atkinson then asked me to describe the vehicle, but all I could tell him was that it was a dark SUV. He responded that there were hundreds if not thousands of SUVs registered in the area and that a busted sign wasn't sufficient evidence to pursue a suspect for possible murder. The detective was right. I was no Sherlock Holmes in the eyes of someone like Atkinson.

We exchanged some more minor questions about the state of Myles' body when I discovered it, and the chance interaction I had with him at Wakefield's Grocery. My internship at the law firm came up, as people knew who my uncle was, especially those in law enforcement. But before Atkinson concluded his interview, he asked one final question.

"Do you ever recall encountering a man named Jordan Mitchell?"

I thought for a moment. Living in Waldo County everyone's name rang a bell it seemed. There were plenty of Mitchells at Belfast High, but none named Jordan. Likewise, if they weren't from here, then the probability got even smaller.

"No, I don't remember meeting someone with that name," I replied softly.

"Thank you, son. You've done a great job. Let us know if there's any more trouble," Atkinson said, handing me his business card. "We appreciate your cooperation, and I'm sorry you had to get involved. Best of luck as an attorney..."

Atkinson then walked out of the house, chuckling slightly at his parting words as he retreated to his truck.

I was glad that it went smoothly. He didn't seem concerned about my preoccupations or whereabouts and likely figured I was straight-laced as a result of being the son of a principal and an accountant, let alone the nephew of a prominent attorney. However, something about his last question, about Jordan Mitchell, got my senses going, leading me to wonder if this truly was the last of my involvement with the incident.

Five

Surprisingly, my sister didn't ask any questions about my encounters with any of the law enforcement officers I met over the weekend. Instead, Lori kept to herself, understanding the gravity of the situation and knowing that I started work tomorrow. She was closer with Myles than any of us, having been a student of his while Mr. Jackson was a long-term math substitute at the high school. Myles served in Iraq, and today was Memorial Day. While he didn't die on the battlefield, there was a sense of conclusion that he was announced dead on this day in particular. The parades in the morning had rightly honored fallen veterans from foreign wars, and yet Myles survived IEDs in Al Anbar only to be killed minutes from his home.

As Monday afternoon went on, news spread online that he had been found this way, which was troubling to many of course given the nature of it all. However, none of the news accounts identified me as the person who found his body. Instead, they just reported that a "beachgoer" or a "local fisherman" had discovered the scene. Mom and Dad recommended we stay off social media, as the burden of knowing part of the story would lead us to become angry with theories or reactions. But most things I had seen were somber.

One man did know a version of the truth, though. That was my uncle. I would report to be his intern in only a handful of hours. According to Dad, Uncle Jack took the news well. He understood my intrinsic curiosity as a future attorney and didn't have the negative reaction that my father expected. So as I began to fall asleep that night, my mind was finally easing up when I realized I hadn't yet responded to Adam's text about another get-together.

Hey! Sounds good, Adam. I'll be there. Where is it?

Megan's house. Lincolnville.
She'll text you the address.

Who else is gonna be there?

Me. Megan.
Her friends from Magdalene. A few more from my high school.
A couple of guys from hockey and their pals.
A typical crowd.

So I know about half the room. Lol.

Bring your sister if you want.

Maybe. We'll see.

Cool. It's okay if you have to go early too.
I gotta get back to Brunswick in the AM anyway as well.

Thanks, man. See you then.

I set my phone back down on the nightstand and clicked the lamp, gazing briefly at the dress clothes I had laid out for my first day. Tomorrow was the first legitimate day of my budding law career. No more haying fields or helping Dad at the office. It felt like I was getting closer to the big leagues.

***

Bakeman & Courtier was one of Midcoast Maine's premier small law firms. My uncle had been an associate at larger firms in Boston and Portland before settling back in the Midcoast, understanding to a degree that it was better to be a big fish in a small pond than vice versa. But as I've said, he also still carried clout in the state and the region, having represented everyone from famous actors to contractors to other small businesses and individuals. His specialty was in asset management and estate planning, though he also had experience with run-of-the-mill things that impacted small towns like land use, family disputes, and criminal defense. Most of that, however, fell on the desk of his partner, Douglas Courtier.

Most folks called Mr. Courtier by his first name Doug. I hadn't seen Doug in years, since Uncle Jack gave us a tour of the renovated Camden office when I was in high school. While I was more interested in what my uncle did, I was looking forward to forging a relationship with Mr. Courtier since it couldn't hurt to have a reference that didn't share my last name.

When I arrived at work, Uncle Jack greeted me and introduced me to their legal secretary, Miss Browning. They called themselves "BBC" for short sometimes in hopes of making her feel included. She was a stunning woman in her late 40's and had been working with Doug and Jack for almost twenty years. They had all practically grown up together here in picture-perfect Camden. I guess she met me once when I was a little kid. Within a few more minutes, he pulled me aside to talk about the incident of the weekend.

"Hey Billy," Jack said. "Your dad told me about what happened. That's horrible. If you need anything let us know. And if anyone gives you bullshit, you remind them who your uncle is, okay?"

"Okay," I chuckled.

"Seriously. I know Atkinson well. He's a good guy, he's helped me in the past with some of our work and he's also been fair when he's wanted to interview clients of ours."

"I'm not worried about the detective," I replied, trying to sound more mature than I knew I was at this stage. "It seems like he has what he needs from me."

"Good. And if anyone in town figures out that you found Jackson and tries to paint a picture of our family – you let me know."

"I will."

"Great. You're a good kid, Billy. I love your passion for truth and justice. We're gonna have a great summer together. And, between you and me, I heard they have a suspect. Don't know any more than that though."

"Good," I said. "That's a relief."

Miss Browning then showed me my desk, and the coffee maker, even joking that Ford & Breen, a bakery on the corner, had better joe if we ever ran out. She explained that my first few days would be organizing case files for the end of the month and putting together briefings for a new client Douglas had just landed. It seemed pretty straightforward, and it didn't take long for the six hours to pass. According to our contract, I couldn't work more than thirty hours per week, which I thought would be plenty to give me the experience I needed while still allowing time for other things. The prospect of taking the LSAT in a year or two didn't bother me, but I still wanted the extra study time this summer to prepare.

Around two o'clock, I prepared to depart for the day, realizing that I would have to wait until some other time to re-acquaint myself with Doug. We would meet later in the week to talk about his new client and the expectations of the case. I shrugged when hearing this from Miss Browning, not wanting to come across as too indifferent or too interested on my first day.

As I walked outside to the street, the fresh air hit me like a train, only emphasizing that the stuffy air inside the law firm had been a bother all morning. The parking spaces along the street were angled and none were vacant, a clear sign that tourist season had begun. Camden, like Belfast, had a bustling downtown. The law firm shared a building with an insurance agency, right near the village green. A large white church shadowed the area near the green, creating a perfect lunch spot. I had spent my previous summers in high school working downtown Belfast and often ate down by the water, but now that I was in Camden I thought I would get used to this new spot as a symbol of a new career. Perhaps one day I'd even work side by side at the firm with Uncle Jack. That would make my family proud. Soon after my late lunch, I did what I do best. I got in my Jeep and traveled Route 1 North back home.

***

The next day seemed to go by faster. I got comfortable working with Miss Browning and prepared for my meeting with Doug. Uncle Jack even invited me to go to lunch at a brewpub in town, so my spot at the village green had to wait another day to truly become a routine. There were no complaints from me, I wasn't about to turn down a free lunch with Uncle Jack. He had some stories to tell, but soon found an interest in my social life toward the end of our meal.

"So, Billy," he said. "Seeing any girls these days or...just hanging?"

I cringed a little.

"No, not seeing anyone," I laughed, gripping my soda.

"That's too bad. I thought maybe you would be coupled up with some other law-school-bound girl from Dartmouth."

I explained that there were a few times when I would go out with someone in Hanover, but nothing major. Our conversation shifted back to the home front, where I mentioned going to a party at Megan LaMarre's home.

"Oh, the LaMarres! You know they're secretly loaded, right? Or should I say not so secret anymore," he added.

"What do you mean?" I asked.

"So you know they used to live in Belfast. Her dad was of course a doctor and the mom co-owned a fitness club."

I nodded.

"Well, he got some promotion down in Portland or something where he worked the past few years. The daughter went with them."

I nodded again. I knew all of this already.

"So eventually the old man cashed in on his inheritance, his new stock options, and his new promotion and they bought a second home up here in Lincolnville for the summers."

"And how do you know this?" I laughed.

"I'm a small-town attorney, bud. We know everything."

"Hopefully I can follow suit," I joked back.

"Someday, Billy. Just wash your car and brush your hair before you go over there tonight. They got a nice place."

Coming from Uncle Jack, who had a nice home of his own, that was saying something. A few minutes later, he paid the check and left a hefty cash tip. Hopefully, this wasn't the last time we shared lunch this summer.

That night, I drove down to Lincolnville to the address Megan gave me. It was odd that they were so keen on inviting me to a house party, but I wasn't going to complain if the LaMarre's place was as nice as Jack described. Lori went with me, as Adam suggested, and it was probably good for her to hang out with us "older kids" a little. She was an old soul, like me, but still likely needed a break from the usual crowd.

When we arrived, we could hear music inside. I carried a 12-pack of Shipyard with me from the Jeep. Lori was still underage, and I promised Mom and Dad I wouldn't let her drink. This was something I would need to deliver on since we were already on thin ice after I lied to them about my trip to Kelly Cove.

Adam greeted us at the door, holding a can of Bud heavy. His friend was nearby, I didn't recognize him but guessed that he was one of the Chamberlain guys. They ushered us to the back porch, and I quickly realized that Uncle Jack wasn't exaggerating as we passed through the house. This home was gorgeous. A huge spacious living room was just after the foyer, with a panoramic window facing the bay. It had hardwood floors and dark blue leather couches, and a massive stone fireplace lay in the center. Above the fireplace, an acrylic portrait of Megan's parents hung in a regal manner. Stairs led to the second floor, with canoe oars used as balusters.

We arrived on the back patio, where I was of course not surprised to see that they also had a swimming pool. Snacks were lining the table, mostly potato chips and various condiments. After a brief lay of the land, Megan appeared next to Adam, and I introduced them to Lori.

"Great to meet you," Megan said cheerfully. "I'm glad you two could make it. We're just gonna chill, play some board games, drinking games, the usual." She laughed again.

"My sister will stick with ginger ale," I joked.

"Okay, we'll see about that," one of the other girls clapped back.

We all spent the next few minutes chatting and gossiping about usual young-adult things: who was shacking up with whom, where people were working, and then some stories about the previous academic year. Adam's friend from Camden named Tim was someone I had met before, so we talked about hockey and golf mainly, not an old rival by any means. The two Chamberlain guys weren't that different from the kids I knew at college.

Before the sunset, a few of the girls, including Megan and Lori, went to the pool while most of the guys stayed back on the patio, sipping our drinks. Adam mixed a mule, and I told him I'd stick to beer since I was driving home. We shared more stories about the glory days and all, most of us having played hockey or another sport. I tried not to check out Megan too much, but it was hard to ignore what was going on by the pool, even if I was in the middle of a conversation about the merits of a four-forward power play.

As it got darker, the girls retreated to the circle where we were sitting, some of them grabbing a hard seltzer or two. I gave Lori a stern look, but nodded, conceding I wouldn't tell if she had only one. Megan was probably on her third or fourth White Claw by now.

We eventually moved inside and sat near the fireplace, with the French doors to the deck still open, a cool breeze complimenting the s'mores and drinks. Adam and his friend decided it was time to play Truth or Dare, with the catch being that someone could take two drinks if they wanted to shift from dare to truth.

I opted for a dare on my first turn. Lori asked me to do a backflip off the diving board. I did, and everyone cheered. I subsequently asked one of Adam's other friends if he would do the same, and he did. We dried off and walked back to the living room where the others had observed. I heard Megan begin her turn, they had bypassed us and gone straight to her.

"This is for everyone..." she started. "What do you think happened to Mr. Jackson? He couldn't have just died in the woods...for real."

There were some immediate whispers among some of the group, but Adam, Lori, and I soon described the situation per the news accounts.

"Maybe he killed himself," one girl said.

"No, he was definitely murdered," another guy retorted.

"Well if he was murdered," Lori asked, glancing over at me. "Then who did it?"

Megan took another sip, peering again around the room before lowering her voice.

"My mom heard that his wife was having an affair," she divulged.

There was some obvious reaction to that statement.

"So you're saying Myles got in a fight with the other guy and he got killed?" I asked.

"Yeah," Megan replied. "Apparently his wife has been sneaking around with one of the dudes from the Percival Estate."

The Percival Estate was a vast Victorian-era mansion in Bayside, and its owners were biotech entrepreneurs from Boston. These people had more money than anyone in town. According to Mrs. LaMarre's story, the rumor was that Myles found out about the affair when Mr. Percival recognized Tracy at the Jacksons' boat repair shop. Supposedly the Percivals were just in to get their cabin cruiser engine replaced. They asked Tracy if she had been at the property recently following their trip out of town. According to the theory, Myles pieced together that she was covertly sleeping with someone who worked at the Percival Estate and confronted this guy, only to be beaten up, shot, and left for dead a few miles away. This all seemed plausible, but also sort of random for a guy like Myles who was so even-keeled. But then again, he had seemed preoccupied on Friday night. The one big logical flaw was that Tracy hadn't simply sought justice already for her dead husband by turning in her new boyfriend. That didn't add up to me.

"And how does your mom know all this?" I asked.

"Oh she gets her hair done with a lady from the courthouse or something, and they were spreading gossip of course."

Typical.

"So this guy shouldn't be hard to find then," Lori suggested.

"Yeah, I bet they'll arrest him soon if this is a legit lead," Adam added.

"Oh for sure. I just can't remember his name."

We all sighed and went back to the game.

As the clock passed midnight, the party broke up for good. Tim and I were putting on our shoes when I noticed he had a nice pair of basketball sneakers.

"Oh, hey, those Jordans are nice," I commented.

"Thanks, bro, I love them."

"That's it!" Megan shouted, her speech still slightly slurred.

"What?" I asked.

"Jordan! That's the killer's name!"

"Okay..." It took us both a second to recognize it.

"And what's his last name?" Adam asked.

"Mitchell. Jordan Mitchell."

The mysterious name that Atkinson had shared with me.

"So why doesn't Tracy just deny the affair and let him rot?" I asked, not holding back.

"It must be more complicated than that," Tim replied.

Tim was right.

Six

Part of me was relieved that the killer had been found. Another part of me was embarrassed for once thinking I could have prevented anything by simply walking in the woods that night. But the last part of me agreed with Adam's friend, Tim. There had to be more to the story. It didn't make sense for Tracy's side boyfriend, this Jordan guy, to kill Myles. If anything, no matter how much we loved Mr. Jackson, it was more plausible that Myles killed Jordan considering the latter was the one secretly messing around with Tracy. There's not a logical precedent in my mind for the *victim* of an extra-marital affair to end up dead. But strong motive or not, it was Mr. Jackson's body that had been found, not Jordan's. His motive to eliminate Myles could have been tied up in romance, the reluctance to break off the marriage, or any other kind of interpersonal struggle. I assumed Atkinson and other cops had already connected those dots.

To my eyes though, Tracy Jackson was the key. She was either the mastermind of the whole thing or an innocent damsel in distress caught in between two warring men, a tale as old as time.

It made sense that the owners of the Percival Estate recognized her as the woman who frequented their property when Jordan was around. However, it didn't make sense that Tracy failed to immediately suspect Jordan when it all unfolded, considering that Myles' body was discovered just miles from the Percival house. After all, an arrest hadn't been made until today apparently and it didn't seem like she turned him in according to Megan's story. But who could be so sure? If Jordan acted alone, he could have hidden the plan to kill Myles from Tracy out of obvious fear that their relationship wasn't strong enough for such a dramatic turn.

On the other hand, Tracy could have decided that the only way to continue her affair with Jordan without telling Myles was to have the latter no longer alive. This happened in the 1990s in Belfast and remained a cold case for years until the wife finally went to jail for using her boyfriend as a hitman against her ex-husband. A situation like that seemed very far-fetched but at the same time, explains why she didn't immediately turn Jordan in to the police since it would have implicated her too. I'd like to think that in either instance, loyalty to a marriage of ten-plus years would supersede all other outcomes, but there was just no getting around the muddiness of the timeline or the hearsay to which I was exposed.

Finally, there was the possibility that none of these scenarios were true. While human nature and the passion for personal relationships could easily have led Jordan to kill Myles, perhaps they were entangled in a deeper struggle surrounding money or power. Maybe Myles had dirt on Jordan beyond just the affair with Tracy. Jordan could have also leveraged his relationship with Tracy to get closer to Myles' business dealings. I frankly had no idea.

But as I continued thinking about it, I kept coming across the same train of thought. In a situation like this where it was almost too complicated to make sense, there was one outcome that stood out in my mind.

While some of these rumors or theories could be true, Myles' death could have been placed on the shoulders of Jordan Mitchell for convenience.

In other words, Jordan could have been framed.

I needed to find out.

***

Work was relatively normal on Thursday despite all the craziness echoing around the area following the weekend's events. Douglas and I had begun to work on a client's suit against the city about zoning or something like that. I was practically just pushing paper and shooting the breeze while he crafted a legal strategy with the client. By the time the day ended, Miss Browning had clocked me as working thirty minutes past when I needed to, but I decided not to tell her or anyone else at the firm that it was because I spent my lunch break looking up anything I could online about the Percivals.

For Marty's birthday that night, the four of us went to dinner down on the water in Belfast, at a place called Neptune's, owned by one of my high school baseball coaches. It was your prototypical seafood restaurant but with a diverse menu. The dining room had numerous nautical motifs and pieces of art, including retired lobster traps hanging from the ceiling and trophy fish molds hugging the wall. A huge trident towered over the bar, an ode to the restaurant's name. Attached to it were mugs for those who came often enough, referred to as "the usuals." Below the display sat a half dozen of its proudest members, settling in for an early start at their bender.

Regrettably, I was worried about someone we knew asking us about the murder of Myles Jackson, understanding that I would need to once again frame my response as I did at the LaMarre's house. So far, neither I nor my sister had uttered a word about the going theory that he was killed over an affair. Likewise, my family knew I had found the body, but there was no public information out there that I did. I intended to keep it that way.

Police announced they had made an arrest yesterday, however, they hadn't released a name yet. I knew it was probably Jordan Mitchell based on Megan's scoop, but frankly, I didn't believe he was guilty anymore. Tonight was about Dad though, so I did my best to not appear preoccupied, a feeling that had become too familiar in the past week. Thankfully, Mom quickly disrupted my chain of thought to break any mental phase I may have been stuck inside.

"Hey Billy, do you mind driving your sister to Molly's tonight?" my mother asked just as the waiter departed to retrieve our check.

"No, of course not," I replied. Molly was a friend of hers who lived just across the Route 1 bridge near Dad's office. It wasn't too much of a detour and I had no plans.

"Great, thanks. Dad and I need to swing by to drop off his car at the shop. He's getting new tires tomorrow."

"Yeah. no problem. I get it, you don't want to go across town and you need your second vehicle." I laughed.

"We all need a fourth one," Lori interrupted with a grin.

We all laughed.

After we left Neptune's, our parents went in one direction while Lori and I took a left to go up the hill toward downtown. My car was parked behind Gillie's, where I was supposed to be on Sunday to watch the Celtics. It wasn't a far walk, but I trailed behind Lori as she had asked for my key.

Suddenly, I heard a man's voice behind me that I didn't recognize.

"William Bakeman," he blurted.

I turned around and saw a man who was probably about forty years old. Shorter like me, with darker hair. He wore a plain black ball cap and a blue denim jacket over a gray raglan tee shirt with olive green corduroys. Evening sunlight disappeared from his face as he turned my way again, so he removed his sunglasses, exposing a clean-shaven face and a youthful curiosity as to what he could learn from me.

"Yes," I replied. Letting my guard down and almost immediately regretting talking to a stranger. However, I didn't want him to follow me and endanger Lori.

"Samuel Wells, DEA." He said, reaching for a badge inside his jacket pocket and showing it to me.

"Okay. What can I do for you?" I asked.

"I think you can help me with something."

"Concerning?" I questioned.

"Myles Jackson."

"I don't know him." Again, I immediately regretted this decision. My brain and conscience were at odds.

"Lying to a federal agent is a felony, son," Wells responded. "Try again."

"Okay, yes. I've met him. But I don't know what you're looking for, you must know he's dead –"

"Yes, I know he's dead," Wells cut me off. "And I also know that you've seen him dead."

I froze.

"Yep. Not every day an Ivy League kid shows up on a police report for something other than public intoxication." Wells added.

I walked toward him more.

"So you just followed me to dinner with my family? I didn't do anything wrong."

"Hey buddy, look, I know you're clean. But I also know you know things and I've got friends who kiss and tell."

"Atkinson sent you?" I asked.

"No," he laughed. "We'll get to who sent me later. For now, I need your help untying this. You clearly know the players."

I nodded. He must have had assistance in finding me from Milton or Lopez.

"Sure, I can help," I said. "But what's a DEA guy doing on a homicide case?"

Wells lowered his voice and looked around.

"William," he said before pausing and speaking again. "I think we both know there's a lot more to this than a love triangle."

I chuckled nervously. Whoever this Samuel Wells from the DEA was, he knew his shit and wasn't just here to dot I's and cross T's like Atkinson and Lopez. He just corroborated the rumor that Megan shared. Like me, he had a desire for the truth and a propensity to distrust others. There was a reason for all of this, and we both knew the public story and rumors didn't pass the smell test.

"Let's do it." I sternly nodded.

"Okay," he handed me a card. "Three o'clock Saturday. Captain's Retreat hotel bar."

"I've been there."

"Great," Wells laughed. "Don't be late."

When I got back to my car. Lori thought I was being coy when I told her I stopped to speak with a friend. My circle needed to be small, even if that meant excluding my sister.

***

By the end of the week, Miss Browning and I had become close pals at the office. She showed me pictures of her grandkids and her pets at the beginning and end of each day. My theory was she knew that I had been involved in the discovery of Myles Jackson and was trying to distract me when I wasn't working on Douglas' case. So far only law enforcement, my immediate family, and Uncle Jack knew I had discovered Myles dead that night, but part of me expected the information to leak over to Miss Browning. To that end, Jack called me into his office at the end of the week, just as we were packing up on Friday.

"Billy!" he shouted. "Come in here! You're not in trouble!"

"Hey Uncle Jack, what's up?"

"TGIF right? Billables and billables all week. Have you met our paralegals yet?"

"No..." I stuttered.

"That's because we don't have any, bud," Jack laughed. "We need them like pigs need the slop. Know anybody?"

"Uh, not around here." I was beginning to wonder where this conversation was going. Even just being here a week, I had put together that the firm was struggling to keep up both financially and with the caseload.

"That's alright. No biggie." Jack leaned back in his chair. A navy Yale banner with white felt hovered above his head, right next to his law school diploma. In the corner of the office was his football jersey from his Andrews College undergrad days. I studied it for a moment, then refocused my attention on his desk.

"When I get back to school in the fall I'll ask around if you want," I suggested.

"Nah, forget about it, Billy. I didn't ask you here for that," he said. Jack then took off his spectacles and sighed. "The word on the street is that the *Press Herald* is running a piece on the Myles Jackson case this Sunday. They have it on good authority that you found him."

"Shit," I replied. This wasn't good news.

"Yeah, exactly," Jack said. "So you're gonna get asked some things by some more reporters unless we can get the *Press Herald* to stand down."

"What do you mean?"

"I know some people down there and can call in some favors."

"Oh, cool," I shrugged.

"Yup. Someone leaked it but I can work something out. Don't worry. You haven't talked to anyone else besides Atkinson and those cops though, right?"

My immediate thought was of course not. But then I remembered Sam Wells last night. Jack didn't need to know about those escapades.

"No, just those guys."

"Great. I can't just read any police report I want but you're definitely in there so that's why it's gonna come out sooner or later."

"So what's the article going to be about?" I asked.

"Mostly a remembrance of his military service and stuff, but they're going to spend a few sentences talking about how he was found."

"Why would a cop leak that much detailed information?"

"Probably to avoid the public discourse changing to how they couldn't find a missing Marine vet miles from his house," Jack retorted plainly. "They'd rather talk about how you found him rather than why they didn't."

The annoyance in his voice was poignant.

"Makes sense," I said.

"Yep. So anyway that's what we're dealing with. Talk to your mom and dad tonight and then we'll come up with a family strategy if things get twisted."

I started to get up and say thank you, reaching for the door before I turned back around.

"Hey. Uncle Jack, one more thing."

"Sure, bud. But hurry 'cause it's Friday night." Then Jack winked.

My gaze met him again as I stepped back into the office.

"Do you think Jordan Mitchell did it? Like, do you think he killed Myles?"

Jack reached for his briefcase and windbreaker.

"Yeah, I do," he replied. Then he lowered his voice. "Major Tom told me the Staties can plant Mitchell in Bayside on Saturday night and they've got a handgun with his prints on it. Matches the wounds from Myles. That's what I've heard."

I raised my eyebrows in curiosity.

"How'd they find him?" I asked.

"A mechanic called about a burglary. They traced Mitchell's truck back to this guy's property with stolen goods, including his sidearm."

"Damn," I whispered.

"Yep. Tom heard it from the Staties. That part will be on the news tonight. Motive is determined to be a domestic *dispute* of some kind." Uncle Jack emphasized the word "dispute" as if to allude to the rumored affair. I pretended not to understand anything about that. And while Chief Milton must have known I found Myles, he wouldn't have leaked to the *Press Herald.*

"Seems like the flow of information is taking forever," I observed. "Five days."

"Yeah you're right, Billy. Myles' wife hasn't been as much help as they hoped."

"Oh," I said, turning back around for the door as we walked out. "That's too bad."

Some of my suspicions were thwarted by the news of the mechanic shop theft linking Mitchell to Myles' murder. Perhaps he wasn't framed. But then on the other hand, Uncle Jack had it on good authority from Tom Milton that the State Police were annoyed with Tracy's sluggish approach, costing them days. So maybe she did know more? Would exposing an affair with her husband's killer send this whole thing into a frenzy? Absolutely. But, if law enforcement already knew, it was only a matter of time before it went public anyway considering all these leaks. To me, and Sam Wells, there was something else at play. I wondered if finding out more about Tracy's story would be a good place to start.

***

One of my greatest strengths, I believe, is not deviating from my original plans. Very rarely do I go rogue and do something to which I haven't yet considered an outcome. Skilled people of the law, who will someday be my bosses, probably look at that as a negative, meaning I do not have the aptitude for the short-term dynamics of dealing with particular cases that require spontaneity and quick thinking. While that was something I hoped to learn from Douglas and Uncle Jack this summer, I was getting a dose of it by being on the front lines of this Jackson murder, even if I wasn't supposed to be. So in theory, I was already getting better at shifting my focus from one thing to another and changing what I planned to do.

For instance, this summer was supposed to be a time of learning from the firm and hanging out with my usual friends on the periphery. Instead, I somehow ended up investigating a murder on the side and reacquainting myself with Adam and Megan. Maybe it was my coming of age, or maybe I desired to get to the truth of a man's disappearance and death—a man whom I had seen hours before his killing. And possibly, my refreshed friendship with AO and Megan was less about my previous attraction to her and more about an inner longing for something different than the usual beers and sports get-togethers I was accustomed to enjoying.

This afternoon in particular, I thought, would be a good day to casually leverage these two developments from the last week against what I had learned from Jack to propel such a strength of mine. There was no reason why I couldn't still be a calculated person, just with new information and a powerful man like Sam Wells in need of my help.

***

Hardman's Dairy Emporium was about a twenty-five-minute drive south, with traffic, from Jack's office in Camden, in a town called Thomaston on the outskirts of Rockland, where I had first seen Megan and Adam a week ago today outside the BMV.

Megan had worked here since the beginning of May, hoping to earn some extra cash this summer like the rest of us. I didn't quite understand why she was working way down here except for the fact that maybe the pay was better or that she knew the owner or something. Nevertheless, it seemed like a good day to come down here and spring Megan for a potential second scoop on Tracy Jackson as well as a scoop or two of ice cream. After all, it was only 2:15 and she had said last week that she wanted to catch up. We didn't get a chance to do that on Wednesday with it being a party and all, so what better time than the present? Hopefully, she hadn't been on her break yet.

When I drove into Hardman's lot, the line was about as long as I expected for a Friday. In the corner of the dirt lot, I saw Megan's blue Bronco right up against the fence on the far side. *Great,* I thought. *She's working.*

I got out of my Jeep and immediately could smell the chocolate syrup and hear the laughter coming from inside the stand. As I stood in line, Megan noticed me and motioned toward the side picnic table away from the crowd.

"Hey Billy!" she shouted as she emerged from the building. "What's up?"

"Uh, just figured I'd swing by as I was in the area."

Not a lie.

"Oh, great. What for?"

"Um, I have to go to the shop soon." I waved my finger in the direction of the row of car dealerships. "Jeep needs work."

Definitely a lie.

"Oh, totally," she said in response. "Thanks for coming by, I was about to go on my break anyway."

Around her apron, I could only see a few ice cream stains from the day's work. Her hair was up in a ponytail and she kept messing with it as we chatted. I heard about Adam's first few days with McGary and we recapped some of the highlights from Wednesday's soiree. Eventually, the subject got to the truth or dare game, and I decided to bring up Tracy's name to her.

"Yeah, that's crazy about Tracy Jackson too," I said, shaking my head.

"Right, my goodness. What a horrible spot to be in. Either you expose your affair with the dude that may have killed your husband or he goes to jail anyway."

"Wait, what do you mean?" I asked.

"My mom's friend also told her that Tracy was with Jordan that night. Like, *with* him that night." She cupped her hands together before continuing. "So this guy has an alibi but probably isn't using it because it will expose the affair."

"That's ridiculous, why don't they just tell the police that?" I asked. "Then everyone finds another way to cover up the affair?"

It again made no sense that Tracy would spare her reputation at the expense of bringing justice to her husband's killer, whether it was Jordan or not.

"Probably because there's enough evidence to the contrary," Megan replied. "He admitted to it when he was arrested anyway, I heard." Megan's mom's friend must have known about the handgun and the mechanic then, I guessed to myself, even if that piece wasn't being made public until tonight.

"Yeah, probably," I replied, content to end it there.

"Sorry, I thought I told you guys." Megan laughed. "Maybe I was too drunk," she laughed again.

"Maybe," I laughed back. Megan glanced at her smartwatch and realized that she probably needed to get back to work. "Hey. Before I go, Adam has a tee time tomorrow at the country club and mentioned that he wanted to invite you. Should I have him text you?"

"What time?" I'd never turn down a round of golf on a Saturday.

"Uh, 2:30 I think."

"Oh shoot, you know what, I can't go. I have, um, family stuff."

And by family stuff, I meant a meeting with Sam Wells. She didn't need to know that though.

"No problem. I'll let him know. We've canceled on you before so now we're even," she laughed again.

"Cool, thanks for the invite though!"

"Thanks for stopping by, Billy." Megan walked away, drifting back toward the building and hopping right back in line to help serve the customers waiting for their ice cream.

Part of me wondered if these patrons even knew about the events that had taken place just a half-hour's drive north last week. Most of them were from far away, I could tell. Straw hats and fanny packs were a clear tell, as were their black SUVs with Massachusetts and New York plates. They resembled kids in a candy store, smitten by our state's beautiful early summer charm and timeless customer service from pretty college kids like Megan LaMarre. Rockland is home to the state's premier lobster festival in a couple of months. Camden is a postcard in real life. Belfast is where you can get craft beer and goat cheese at the same storefront. Our towns were tourist havens.

And yet the most charming of all, our little village of Bayside, where I would be returning to soon, was the site of Maine's most recent homicide, likely unbeknownst to these folks who traveled up I-95 looking to find something tranquil in their lives.

By seeking the truth, I realized that I could threaten such a caricature of this unique place; that a reputation which was only challenged in jest by an occasional newspaper column or blog post, could very well be unmasked by whatever I discovered. However, in weighing my ambition with the possible consequences, the truth had to be my true north.

Seven

Saturday morning, I slept in about as much as a guy my age could, which was well past ten o'clock. Thankfully my parents didn't give me a hard time about it, probably because they knew I had a tough week. We were sort of at that weird time. In theory, they couldn't nag me about that stuff anymore because I was 21 years old, yet I still lived at their home during the summer.

My biggest conflict was to figure out if I was going to tell them about my meeting with the DEA agent. Over the last few days, they had minded their own business with the entire situation. Even when last night's news broke that Jordan Mitchell had stolen mechanical equipment and used it to kill Myles, our family didn't even talk about it. In my mind, they were ready to move on from the whole thing, likely out of fatigue and sadness combined. After all, it was Mom who had worked with Myles back when she was a classroom teacher and he was a substitute. Word had it that the school was going to do something to honor his memory at graduation, but a new policy enacted last year by the school had prevented them from doing so. All mourning was to be private or orchestrated by the victim's family. And in this case, we knew Tracy was all clammed up.

As the mid-afternoon approached, Mom and Dad were out doing errands and Lori was with friends when I decided I should leave and be early for my "appointment" with Wells. For a Saturday afternoon, the weather put a literal damper on what would normally be a bustling town, now that we were well past the unofficial kick-off to summer. When I drove past the Bayside Golf Club, a few miles from my house, the parking lot was unusually bare and there weren't many people out and about in the foggy links.

My travels then took me onto Route 1, heading north or east depending on your final destination. To get to the hotel that Sam was staying at, I had to cross the Passagassawakeag River on the Route 1 Bridge once I bypassed Belfast proper. The view from high above the river was generally a magnificent one, especially when the bay was littered with sailboats and moorings. On a typical day, I would look down to see those vessels dotting the harbor with other small craft circling. A large modern shipyard had been built about a decade ago and attracted yachts from around the world in the summer. Pedestrians flocked the footbridge to catch a glimpse of the occasional harbor seal or try their best at mackerel fishing where the river met Belfast Bay. Marty usually took humor with those people, as he called the structure "No Fish Bridge." The river was itself aptly named "Passy" by locals, though its origins ironically came from a Native American description of a good place to catch sturgeon. In my eyes, this vantage point of the town was the best of all. There was nothing better than a bustling waterfront in the warmer months.

This afternoon was different though, and the area had an unsettling calmness to it, almost like it was a simmering pot getting ready to boil over. I hoped that what I was about to do was unrelated to that eerie feeling.

Eventually, after passing Dad's office building and a handful of seasonal businesses along the corridor, I hit my right-hand turn signal, entered the hotel parking lot, and reared the Jeep into a spot near the building. Over the years, this place had been called by several different names before some real estate conglomerate bought it from a hotel chain and turned it into a vast inn called The Captain's Retreat. If you asked me, it still looked like any old hotel you'd see along the highway, even if the interior decor was modified to be trendier.

When I walked inside, I turned left to head down the corridor toward the tavern and bar area. The dampened afternoon light cast a glare over the dark wood tables, making it difficult at first to see which patrons were seated where. My eyes quickly adjusted and I gathered my senses to assess the room. On the wall, there were nautical and wartime-themed artifacts that told a story of Maine's decorated past. Like Neptune's, the bar had an assortment of mugs hanging from the ceiling. Horse racing was on the television. Finally, in the far corner, underneath a hallowed canoe-turned-chandelier, sat a man with his back to the entrance. I recognized this man as Sam Wells and moseyed my way over, smiling at the hostess and telling her I was joining a friend.

I soon joined Sam in the booth. He wore a faded Red Sox cap and casual clothing - a golf shirt and jeans, doing his best to blend in with the customers I suppose. He slid me a drink menu as I sat down.

"Order what you want, Billy. Drinks on me. We're gonna be here for a bit."

It was the first time in my life that a true adult had said this, let alone without a greeting first to warm me up.

"Thanks," I replied, pulling the menu closer to me.

"Nobody followed you, right?" Sam asked.

"Not that I know of, no," I said, pleasantly alarmed to have met someone more paranoid about this than me.

"Alright, well if anyone comes in and looks shady, you get up and go to the bar. That's our signal."

I nodded.

"Listen," Sam continued, "This thing is a whole lot more real than you know right now. And I'm going to need your help to get this done. I've staked my career on it."

"No pressure," I retorted.

He cracked a smile and continued again. "I'm also gonna be straight with you because I need you to trust me for this to work. You're my best chance now, believe it or not."

I nodded back again.

Then Sam sighed and lowered his voice, looking over his shoulder.

"Jordan Mitchell didn't kill Myles Jackson. I am certain of it," he said quietly.

"How do you know?" I replied, puzzled, moving closer.

"I know because while Mitchell ain't exactly Saint Peter, he also isn't a murderer. Mitchell didn't do as much as touch a cigarette his whole life. He also doesn't need the money. The Percivals have given him all he ever needs. So drugs, cash - none of it is his forte. He's not motivated by them."

"So then what do drugs and cash have to do with Myles Jackson?"

"I have it on good authority that Jackson knew about a high-profile drug syndicate out of Saint John," Sam paused, "in Canada."

My eyes widened.

"But it ain't your normal drug ring. According to my source, the Canadians have contacts here in Eastern Maine that can move contraband anywhere they want using means that not even us guys at the DEA can catch up with yet. Sheriffs have been chasing them for months. They've got enough fentanyl in their network to wipe out the whole state and more."

He continued telling the story, and we only paused once more, when the bartender brought me a Belgian-style wheat beer on draft. Chances are I would want one more by the end of this conversation.

About a month ago, Sam met someone who knew about the scheme. This person knew Sam had connections in Maine, including an ancestor who was once Maine's governor. He also learned that Sam had career ambitions and approached him to take on the case of uncovering the syndicate, worried about Myles and his safety. Sam's supervisors in Boston gave him the green light and allowed him to move up here for the summer.

Sam told me he learned that Myles was asked to build a special cargo hold for the syndicate but had refused. The Maine cartel wanted to be able to secure and transport drugs within the Gulf of Maine and the Bay of Fundy without needing to commandeer a larger vessel and was thus testing how feasible it was to have a special hold built into recreational seacraft that couldn't be seen from above water. They hoped to recruit mariners to transport their products. The cartel also knew Myles was a skilled boat builder and had knowledge of modern technology from his military days. Myles refused and this is where things went south. The local runners told their Canadian friends and up the chain it went. If Myles wasn't going to cooperate, he was going to become a loose end.

The Friday before the holiday weekend, Sam attempted to contact Myles but got no answer. I shared with Sam that I witnessed him pick up a call that night, and his reply was uncanny yet comical, to say the least.

"I know he got a call while standing beside you," Sam laughed. "You don't think I saw that on the grocery store CCTV?"

"Didn't think about that," I admitted, shaking my head. Sam continued.

According to his story, it was that night when Sam became interested in me as a secondary source of information, but he told me things went nuclear the next evening when his office got the missing persons alert for Myles. It was at that moment when Sam suspected Myles was eliminated by someone involved in the syndicate. Someone had beaten Sam to the punch, and in his opinion, it couldn't have been Jordan Mitchell.

Later that weekend, when Sam learned that *I discovered the body*, Sam concluded that I would be a good asset to him. Right after the server left for our second round, I asked Sam how he knew of this cartel, and he began telling me how they came to be.

Eight

Sam continued, stirring what looked like an Old-Fashioned with a small wooden stick. He looked around the room discreetly once more and then began telling the story of the syndicate's origin.

About fifteen years ago, Maine's drug crisis took center stage politically when the issue of our opioid epidemic was debated in the halls of Augusta and on local news. Oxycontin was the drug talked about most commonly, because of its national familiarity. At the same time, the merits or lack thereof regarding recreational pot were also being debated along with what to do about widespread heroin use. There was a time when that's all that people talked about. Oxy got the documentaries and news headlines for a while, then the debate over weed, but, in the backdrop of it all, a more lethal drug was emerging regionally: fentanyl.

How it got here was even more of a political hot-button, but naturally, one way it arrived on our coasts was via smugglers who operated internationally with their local cartels, mainly via Mexico but also from Canada. So, by the time I was in high school, almost everyone knew it was becoming a problem in our communities. Sam's DEA Office in Boston and their counterparts here in Maine were on the lookout for the traffickers constantly, and, for the most part, did the best job they could given the circumstances.

Though Sam soon told me that one of their white whales was a man by the name of Conrad Kidd, who, by every possible measure, had to be the cartel leader in Eastern Maine. They believed he was the same man who worked with the Canadians to get thousands of grams of fentanyl into the state each year in return for a big payday. However, they couldn't figure out who he reported to if anyone, or discover enough evidence to locate him or to bring him in as an alleged trafficker. The truth was, Kidd was too savvy to snag.

Sam's theory was threefold. First, he believed that if Conrad Kidd was a key component of the syndicate, he must report to someone in New Brunswick who was helping get the drugs past both Canadian and American authorities. Sam had tried working with officials in Canada but the evidence just wasn't amounting to anything substantial and the Canadians started to think Conrad wasn't a lead to their gatekeeper at all.

Second, regardless of whether Conrad Kidd was linked to the Canadian cartels, he must have been operating in Maine long enough to set up a local network of his own as part of a larger syndicate. He had grown up in New Hampshire but spent his whole adult life in Eastern Maine so far and was an oyster farmer by trade. Those businesses were probably a front by now since the real money was in trafficking. Sam believed that we needed to uncover other members of the network before we could get Conrad Kidd.

The third component of his theory revolved around Jordan Mitchell's innocence rather than his presumed guilt. Sam believed Jordan had been compromised by the cartel and that Conrad had gotten to him, leveraging Jordan's relationship with Tracy Jackson as a means to frame the murder of Myles Jackson on him rather than somebody within the cartel. Then, Sam believed, the admission of guilt by Jordan was a signal to the cartel to let him and Tracy be uninvolved going forward on the condition that if no one talked, no one else would be hurt. I generally agreed with this part of his theory, since the loose motive of a romantic entanglement had not set well with me since day one and that suspicion was frankly the only reason for my continued interest in this whole thing. However, neither one of us could square why there wasn't a continued effort by local law enforcement to look deeper into Mitchell after his easy surrender. Unless, of course, they just wanted the whole thing to go away because it was a stain on the community.

Finally, as the conversation started to wind down, the drinks stopped flowing. I had capped it at two anyway since I had to drive home. Sam Wells opened up to me with his theories in a way that I didn't expect during just our first meeting. Like me, he believed that Jordan wasn't the real killer, despite the mounting public evidence. Like me, he believed that Myles deserved true justice, but not at the expense of an innocent man, but rather a guilty party led by Conrad Kidd. Knowing the backstory of these three men was bound to put my life in danger at some point, but so was the cost of doing what was right. I could be headed straight into a storm.

Later, the server left with Sam's credit card, and Sam began to pull out his wallet. I wondered how a man like him ended up in the shadows of the DEA, to begin with. For a guy who looked like a *GQ* model, why wasn't he off in Silicon Valley somewhere founding a startup with a ten-figure net worth and a third house in Cabo? Or, why wasn't Sam Wells a high-ranking intel officer in the Agency or something?

He noticed my facial expression and smiled.

“You want to know why I’m here, right?” he asked, motioning his head toward the window and the bay. “Like, in rinky-dink hill-billy Maine with you solving a murder case?”

I chuckled, then nodded.

“Well,” he continued. “My ancestors are from Maine. I love this place. Spent summers coming up to the coast to fish or boat with my dad,” then he paused. “My father was at the Pentagon on 9/11. He was my age at the time, roughly. We had moved from Mass’ and were living in the D.C. area while I was in high school - an Episcopalian prep school in Virginia. But after 9/11, I knew I wanted to get into law enforcement. Seeing those guys - and the firefighters - rescue people. It was an inspiration.”

“Wow, did your dad survive?”

“Yes, he was a non-defense department employee so he was only there for a quick meeting. Very brief stint but at the worst time. We were lucky,” Sam trailed off.

I shook my head.

“Then,” he continued. “We moved back to Boston and I went to the Police Academy. Could have gone to Harvard Business but that’s what I wanted to do. Serve people. My dad taught me that. At the Academy, I graduated near the top of my class, right around the time *The Departed* came out. That was interesting.”

We both laughed. “It gets better,” he said. “About eight or nine years into my career my partner and I were in Watertown participating in the manhunt for the Boston bombers. At that point, I felt like the guy who survived the *Lusitania* and the *Titanic*.”

I looked back outside, then back at him, and shook my head again, digesting it all.

"Yes," Sam said. "I know I still haven't answered your question." He paused again. "After the whole Marathon situation, I was introduced to a man at the DEA's New England Division and he recruited me to be a special agent. I told him I'd join but didn't want to serve anywhere other than the Boston area. I wasn't going back to D.C."

"Makes sense," I said.

"Yep, so I've been there over ten years now. The fentanyl crisis is my focus. Too many kids - or people your age - die of this shit. It's horrible and I'm going to do something about it."

I nodded.

"We used to think that the biggest threats were bombers and hijackers," he said, alluding to his past. "Then it was oxy on the drug level. And those are still huge threats, don't get me wrong. But right now, there's so much crap coming through under our noses and we have to stop it," Sam paused again and looked back out the nearby window before continuing.

"Here, in this beautiful place, there should be no excuse not to keep our communities safe from drugs this bad. I love it too much to let that happen. That's why I took on the case. I just wish the locals would help me out so I wouldn't have to resort to college kids."

I laughed.

"No offense," he added.

"None taken," I replied with a grin.

"So, that's where we are. I'm glad you asked. We must know each other if we're gonna work together on this."

"Right," I said. "You've been a lot more helpful to me than the other cops. My uncle told me that one of them was going to leak to the press that I was the person who found Myles Jackson."

"Well," Sam said. "He was right. I think one of them did, but I wouldn't call myself a cop."

I looked back at him with a confused look.

"I was going to tell you this too, and I need to be honest with you. It was me who created that narrative so that you would help me."

"What?!" I exclaimed, trying not to make too loud of a noise. We were still in the booth.

"Don't worry. The press doesn't know anything. But I know you trust your uncle so I had one of my guys pose as the *Press Herald* and give him a call."

"Unbelievable," I muttered.

"Yeah, hey, I was worried you would get cold feet. Therefore I had my guys create and then extinguish the narrative fast enough for your uncle to not get too spooked. I gambled that if you were worried about your name coming out, you would still help me. It worked, and when your uncle thought he called down to Portland, he actually reached us and we backed off. Some attorney," Sam smiled.

"What the hell, man," I sighed.

"This is what we're gonna have to do, Billy. We're getting creative. I can't play by the book up here."

"Alright, so tell me one thing while we're being honest: Who told you I found the body? Who was your source for that?"

"Nobody told me," Sam replied. "I was in our Portland annex on Sunday morning and I looked at the security tape of Wakefield's after the FBI got the bulletin for Myles. That was his last credit card transaction."

"Okay..."

"And I saw you on the tape. Our guys ID'd you as just some random citizen who saw him. Nothing more. State and local agreed. Then on Sunday night, the county sheriffs had you as the person who found the body and people started getting squirrely for a second, but that was found to be premature when Jordan's name came up. Atkinson cleared you too. The police report on you was brief, but I did some digging and realized that you were way too smart to not be of use to my case."

"What do you mean?" I asked.

"Well, the only reason I ever got involved was because I knew Myles Jackson had info on the syndicate. My involvement with police procedural work on the murder is arbitrary from a jurisdiction point of view. The bosses in Boston just care that I can use it to nail the cartels. And as far as the local authorities are concerned, they have their guy, so we have to operate a little differently. Your family - and your family friends - are influential, but I know they don't want a fed sniffing around. You, on the other hand, are like me. You're aiming for something higher."

"So, then who told you about Myles?" I asked, trying not to pry too much.

Sam lowered his voice.

"I care about your safety, and theirs. We'll get to that, I promise."

Sam patted his hand on the table and got up, waving goodbye and disappearing down the hall back toward the guest rooms. I followed but turned right toward the door and went back to my Jeep.

My gut still trusted this guy, even after the charade involving Uncle Jack and the newspaper. He had risked too much in his life to be using me for something besides the truth. I wondered why Milton, Lopez, Atkinson, and the other folks involved were content to see Jordan go to jail without any further investigation of the situation. Perhaps his bizarre admission of guilt was enough for them to move on and continue their already difficult jobs. I had tremendous respect for law enforcement and the law, which is why I wanted to be an attorney. However, at what cost would this respect and pursuit of the truth be worth it? I was already lying to my family and my new friends. Sam seemingly gave up a life on the beach or Wall Street when he was my age to fight crime all over the East Coast. Part of me wondered if I was facing a similar choice.

Nine

Over the next few weeks after that afternoon with Sam, things appeared very normal. I continued working at the firm. Lori got a job waiting tables at another seafood restaurant in Belfast. Mom got out of school for the summer and Dad got through quarter two. Uncle Jack and I shared more lunches. Miss B and Doug got to know me better. Adam and I watched the Stanley Cup together at Gillie's, or another spot depending on the day and our schedules. He and Megan even invited me to a few more parties at their houses and such. Summer life in Maine was beginning, and soon, the community also started to heal from the initial shock of Myles Jackson's death. There were memorials and tributes and almost everyone, except for those like me who had a vested interest, began to move on from the tragedy. We didn't hear as much about Jordan Mitchell anymore either, and his lawyers rarely spoke publicly anyway. Life soon passed it all by.

Under the surface though, Sam insisted that he and I continue to meet a couple of times a week at various locations in person, choosing to never communicate via text message, phone, or email. Typically, I would meet him under the guise of going for a run or taking a drive with friends. Nobody in my family ever asked. Adam, Megan, and our growing group of summer friends didn't notice when I left parties early. Sam and I were able to go over some of the details I had picked up from work, mostly just hearsay I heard at work about court proceedings. Jordan's trial was set for September. Beyond that, I felt like I wasn't much help to Sam. He wanted to nail Conrad's men, but as time went on the two of us desperately needed a breakthrough to prove it. Each day that the world in and around Bayside returned to normal, the real killers were one day closer to never being caught.

***

The firm was closed on the Fourth of July, my first real weekday off since Memorial Day, as I spent most of Juneteenth with Dad fixing his lawnmower again. There had been a lot of water under the bridge since that weekend in late May. To everyone else, we had reached peak Maine summer, but to me, I was still stuck thinking about events almost six weeks prior.

The morning of the Fourth, I woke up and slipped on a pair of board shorts and an old Patriots tee shirt. There was no need to dress up, even though our house was hosting the cookout this time. On Memorial Day Weekend we were at Jack and Bonny's. In September we would be at Scott & Aunt Lori's. We hadn't yet figured out a tradition for June. My guess is when I had kids it would end up being my house since I was the oldest grandchild. That was a thought for another day, though.

When I got downstairs, I put on some flip-flops and rode down to the beach on my bike. Bayside had a few beaches, but Kelly Cove was the most convenient. It also happened to be the place where I discovered Myles. Today though, I wanted to go down there and start the day before the hustle and bustle of the cookout kicked in and before my parents asked me to help set up.

After arriving there, I leaned my bike up against the guardrail and trotted down to the sand. It was an unusually calm morning on the bay, so I decided to stick my feet in the water. This was no Caribbean or South Pacific, as the water felt ice cold on my toes, even for July. I watched a few crabs traipse around my feet. Then, my phone vibrated and I pulled it out of my pocket, careful to not accidentally drop it in the ocean.

It was Lori.

Where are you?
Mom wants us to run to town to get some last-minute stuff.

I took a bike ride, I'll be right back.

The fun was over, or something. I put my shoes back on and jogged up to my bike, taking one last look at the beach before I rode away. It was impossible to come here now and not think of finding a dead body. The flashbacks and second guesses were on a loop every time. I shook my head and peeled back up the road toward home, cursing this place the whole way.

Mom and Dad were cranked about hosting the cookout, despite doing so once a year for two decades, but I understood. Thankfully, the same cast of characters, minus Chief Milton and one of the distant cousins, showed up so we were able to pick right back up where we left off. The absence of Major Tom probably meant no random surprises this time, I thought, and for once, I was right. It was about as normal of a cookout as possible. I even convinced my little cousins, who I usually never interacted with, to play wiffle ball. Toward the end of the day, Lori came over to where I was sitting with a beer.

"Hey Billy, can you drive me to Camden for the fireworks?"

I laughed and raised my beer can as if to say I wasn't driving anywhere.

"No, but you can take my keys," I said.

"Really?"

"Sure thing, just not a scratch!" I shouted.

"I promise!" she replied, matching my emphatic tone.

That night, after I low-key sobered back up, I sat down on the sofa to watch the Boston Pops Fireworks on Channel 2. It wasn't uncommon for somebody down in Bayside or across the bay in Islesboro to light real ones off, but I still enjoyed the TV display, especially if one of my favorite bands was performing. Part of me regretted not hanging out with Adam and Megan, who had also invited me to the Camden fireworks, or going with my sister, even if she drove. Perhaps it was the beer talking when I said I would be a hermit tonight. A few hours into the night, Lori returned home, busting through the door.

"Thanks, Billy, it was a lot of fun. My friends think you're the coolest brother ever."

She could be genuine and sarcastic at the same time. I appreciated that.

"Great, glad you had a good time," I replied.

"Your friends were there too, I saw them."

"Oh neat," I muttered, reaching for the remote to lower the volume.

"Yeah, but if I were you, I'd be happy I didn't go," Lori rebuked.

"What do you mean?"

"Well, the boyfriend there, hockey guy..."

"Adam?" I interjected.

"Yeah, Adam Olsen. He and Meg got pretty heated there for a second. I happened to hear them from where we were. No cap."

"What were they arguing about?" I asked, out of genuine curiosity.

"I couldn't hear exactly, but she kept saying how he's working too much."

"At the Senator's office?"

"Yeah," Lori said. "I can only assume. Hey Billy, maybe it's your chance to swoop in, she clearly has affection for you if she wants you to always hang out with them."

"Yes. Lori. I am going to believe that Megan likes me so much that she asks me to hang out with her boyfriend as the third wheel."

The elder Bakeman sibling was not as skilled with sarcasm.

"Suit yourself," my sister retorted, walking up the stairs. "I won't say 'I told you so.'"

It was time to go to bed, for America's sake.

xxx

Thursday night, the day after the Fourth, my family and I went out for dinner in Lincolnville at a lobster shack my folks adored. In the summer, the place was almost always packed, so a post-holiday outing was likely to be tricky. Sure enough though, we were seated with a minimal wait.

Dad ordered a full bug, Mom the fish and chips, Lori a chicken wrap, and me a fried seafood platter. It was like old times, before this whole mess, and everyone seemed happy to spend some time together on an unusual off night for Lori at work. I had put aside our squabble from the night before. After we were all done eating, I got up to use the men's room when I noticed Megan of all people outside waiting on the bench near the entrance. I walked outside in that direction, figuring it would not only be rude to ignore her but also understanding that I might be able to conclude what her argument with Adam was about.

She quickly noticed me when the noise of the door behind me closing got her attention. I smiled and waved, and she motioned over. I suppose the bathroom could wait.

"Hey, Billy - what're you doing here?" she asked.

I tilted my head back toward the restaurant. "Family night out, I suppose."

"Cute. That's fun. Adam was supposed to show up and meet me here for our night out, but it's almost seven and he's gonna end up being an hour late."

"Oh, sorry to hear that," I said. It was unlike him to be late since like me, he grew up going to rinks at six in the morning.

"Yeah, it's whatever. I'm sure there's a reason."

"Totally," I added. "Have you tried calling him?"

Dumb question, I thought immediately.

"Mmmhmmm," she nodded, looking down at her phone once more. Her elbows had made red spots on her otherwise tan legs. She tried to rub them out but couldn't, frustrated it seemed about the whole evening.

"Well, I hope Adam comes by. If not and you get bored, we can always hang out when I'm done here as long as you don't mind driving me back to Bayside. We took one car."

"Alright, Billy. Thanks," she smiled back. "Your sister would probably tease you for that. Having a girl drive you home?"

"Well for your case, and maybe mine, I hope you don't have to use me as a last resort."

"Geez, you're an attorney already," she laughed before trailing off again. "I just don't understand why he's bailing again."

"Again?" I asked.

"Yes, counselor," she chuckled before getting serious again. "He's bailed on me all summer, even tried to do it on the Fourth."

"I never noticed, we have hung out in the big group so much," I muttered, understanding that this had to be the situation that Lori described for me yesterday.

"Yeah, it all started that night we were supposed to be at his cousin's in Bayside."

I looked back at her, puzzled. There must have been another party there I wasn't invited to since they had asked me to join one of them that day at the BMV.

"Oh, wow, so back before we started hanging out," I said.

"No, it was the night we were gonna have you come by but then his aunt came back early apparently," Megan explained.

"Wait, so you didn't go to the movies that night?"

"No. We were supposed to, but Adam ended up ditching me for his cousin or something. I didn't care at the time but then it became a pattern. He's great, but lately, it's just been so predictable."

"Oh, I'm sorry."

"No, I'm sorry, I shouldn't be bombarding you with this drama. You should be hanging out with your family."

I shook my head. "Don't be sorry," I croaked, trying to piece everything together in my head.

"Alright," she said. "I'll text you in a couple if he doesn't show."

"Okay," I said, turning back toward the restaurant. "See ya."

She waved.

Lori was right about them arguing last night and Megan seemed legitimately pissed at Adam. But beyond all the soapiness of this budding triangle, there was a more important matter to me at least.

Why did Adam and Megan lie to me about their whereabouts and actions on the night of Myles' disappearance? If they didn't go to the movies, and he ditched her, where did she go? Where did he go? Why had they kept that story together on subsequent occasions since? Were they hiding something from me?

On one hand, they didn't owe me shit. They were their own couple, and God only knows I've kept things from them these past several weeks. Though on the other hand, I had gathered secrets at their and others' expense to protect the pursuit of what I believed was the truth. Had their secrets been cultivated to hide that same truth? It was a loose connection to make, but the last time I had a hunch, a dead body appeared at my feet. My instinct kicked in again, and I decided to show up somewhere I probably wasn't welcome, The Captain's Retreat Inn.

Ten

I didn't tell my folks where I was going, because I didn't want to lie. After the whole situation with not going to Gillie's back in May, I think my parents let me live my life considering I was an adult now, as long as I didn't end up dead in a brook too. If they asked, I would cross that bridge when I got there, literally.

On the other side of the Passagassawakeag, I pulled up to the inn and parked in the same spot. When I arrived at the front desk, I asked for Sam Wells, Room 222. They phoned up to him, and I met him down in the lobby.

"Billy, what the hell are you doing here? There could be bad ears anywhere this time of day."

"Listen, Sam. We have a breakthrough. I think."

His eyes widened.

"Go on," he nodded.

"Adam Olsen, my friend, lied to me about where he was the night Myles disappeared. And his girlfriend, Megan, has been complaining about him working too much."

"This the girl you knew before?"

"Yeah, I've known both of them for a few years."

"Alright, and so what?" Sam itched where his black ball cap had been all day.

"He's a congressional intern, I replied. "What the hell would he be doing? Especially with holidays every other week?"

"Well, he's an ambitious try-hard like you, right?"

"Yeah.." I started.

"Okay then, I still don't see how you are connecting him to our case. Some kids are bickering and they didn't share their plans with you. So what."

"Why lie to me? I didn't mean anything to them at that point, there was no need…" I trailed off before starting again. "She was pissed, Sam. Like on another level. And I think that's why she spilled the beans by accident."

"Billy, look, I gotta question your judgment here. It's too much of a stretch. Plus, these people are rich folks, they're not who we look at. No motivation."

"Haven't you seen enough unlikely villains in your career?" I asked, my voice raising a little.

"Sure, Billy. I have. But your friends aren't gonna lead us to Conrad Kidd. They're not even in the same stratosphere."

Sam peered off past me to some spot on the wall, then sighed. "And you need to square right away if you would rather get in her pants or find the truth."

Honestly, someday I wouldn't mind both, but I shook my head. Sam was right. They could have just wanted to protect my feelings the first night they canceled on me, especially if AO truly wanted to be my friend. Megan was a nice girl too. It wasn't Megan's fault that her boyfriend had been standing her up all summer. While difficult to separate, I decided to compartmentalize their relationship and our friendships from the task at hand with Sam.

But at the same time, I wondered if I could still use one as leverage for the other. In other words, could the crack between Adam and Megan be a gateway to learning more about the mystery surrounding Jordan Mitchell, Conrad Kidd, and Myles Jackson? Surely if Megan was being stood up by Adam, she would be more likely to confide in a friendly face like me about most things, including the rumors she was hearing from her parents' friends. After all, Megan was the one who told me about Jordan Mitchell to begin with. And, if she was spending more time alone, I could continue to gently use her openness to my and Sam's advantage.

This scheme was not in my typical friendship playbook. I was a loyal person and would certainly be using her if I never read her into what I was doing. But, if I confided in her the way she confided in me, I would have to tread carefully to bear in mind both her safety and Sam's trust in me. Ultimately, this was all beginning to be as much of an exercise in trust and loyalty - to my town, my friends, and my family - as it was a pursuit of justice for Myles Jackson and Jordan Mitchell.

The rest of the day, I didn't speak to anyone about anything. I was too lost in my thoughts. That was a normal occurrence for me but I tried not to let it show to anyone else. Dad and I watched the Red Sox on TV, like usual, and it wasn't until I went up to my bedroom following the game's conclusion that I decided to make a move.

If I was going to use Megan, arguably the kryptonite of my past feelings, should there be one in the world, then I would need to keep her boyfriend on my side too. Adam was indeed a friend of mine and someone with whom I shared mutual trust. I couldn't get away with chatting up his girlfriend more than usual without him continuing to believe that I was harmless romantically, especially considering he and Megan were at odds lately. And despite what my sister and mom believed, and my initial reaction to Sam's comment, that was the truth at this particular moment in time. It may not have been true three years ago and it may not be true forever, but it is now. Thus, Adam's trust in me was paramount.

However, like with Megan, I still wasn't going to loop him in on my work with Sam Wells. If it ever came out unintentionally, I could always shut off communication with both of them or explain that Sam had finished the case without me and that I was done. I didn't think Sam would care either way. I think he was looking for me to take a risk based on our conversation at the hotel.

When I sat down on my bed, I reached for my phone and texted Adam. The home run derby was on TV tomorrow night and would be the perfect cover for a casual meet-up.

Gillie's Monday night? Home run derby?

It didn't take him long to reply.

Sure thing boss, beers on me.

Perfect. If AO bought the beers, then it wouldn't look like I was buttering him up.

***

On Monday morning I arrived at work to find a stack of papers on my desk higher than Mount Katahdin. I guessed that either my uncle or Doug had come in over the weekend to work late on a case and decided to load me up with research this week. The first few documents looked like construction code, so my week was stacking up to be long already. Thankfully, I had beers at Gillie's to look forward to tonight.

But around ten o'clock, Doug came storming into the entryway and headed straight for my uncle's office, clearly upset about something. I hoped it wasn't my fault. Without even looking at me or Miss B, he shut Jack's door and closed the shades.

Miss B and I exchanged looks. Not a good sign.

They weren't shouting at one another, but I knew from experience hearing my dad and Jack argue that there wasn't always a need to when he knew he was getting his point across. For about ten minutes, I sat there at the little desk in silence, failing to care at all about what the state allowed when a business wanted to close a section of the road.

Just as I was about to get up for coffee, Doug opened the door and motioned me into Jack's office. I sat down in the corner and fiddled with the chair while Jack stood up.

"Doug and I have a case that's gonna demand more work from us," my uncle declared, brushing muffin crumbs off of his shirt. "It's going to end up making you do some extra leg work on the side for our other cases, like research and file prep. It'll be good for you but we want to know if you think you can do it."

"I think so," I replied. "So far the stuff I've done is manageable."

"Great, and we're going to have you work eight to four starting next week and raise your stipend. One more scheduled off day per week too. We'll call it a family Christmas gift if we have to."

"Thank Uncle Jack," I relaxed. "Means a lot."

On one hand, professionally this was great news, but on the other, it meant more work here and fewer things elsewhere, including investigating with Sam.

"We're happy to have you here this summer," Doug said. " I can't believe it's already half-over."

"Same," I sighed.

"We don't want you to sacrifice too much, too soon," Jack interjected. "But it is part of the deal, which you'll learn eventually."

I laughed and nodded.

"And it's not like a college kid wants to spend his summer partying and hanging with chicks anyway," Doug added.

Or working with the DEA to solve murders and drug trafficking. I thought

"Nah," my uncle said, "Billy's a good kid and Megan LaMarre will understand."

I blushed.

"We know she's who you've been leaving to go see, buddy," Jack laughed. "No need to hide it, you're among friends and family."

I laughed too and shook both of their hands, thanking them again.

If they only knew.

***

Gillie's Sports Bar was the kind of joint that seemed archetypical but was unique to those who truly paid attention. Upon entering, two rounded booths were flanking the door and shaped two-hundred and seventy degrees. It was the ideal spot to catch teachers and friends' parents drinking on a Friday night. Partially because behind those booths were two large windows, facing Main Street. You didn't even have to go inside to see the Millers and Tom Collins' flowing night after night.

The bar was on the right side of the main room, with several large television screens mounted above, where I would've been watching the Celtics the night I found Myles Jackson. To the left were booths and high tops, my favorite place to sit, each one surrounded by memorabilia dating from Bobby Orr to Robert Parish to Mookie Betts and of course Tom Brady. These things made Gillie's not unlike any other sports dive in New England, but the architecture and layout allowed the place to carry on in the twenty-first century even if its primary frequenters may have peaked in the Nineties.

Tammy, one of the bartenders who knew our family, was still surprised each time that I was already of age. She came to the end of the bar to greet me when I walked in, but I motioned my hand toward the high tops and told her I was meeting a friend. She insisted to her coworker that she serve us anyway, and told me she'd be right over.

I met Adam at the corner table, he had already started a tab before I arrived. He clutched a Moose Lager with one hand and his phone in the other, checking his Snapchat. When I pulled out the chair, he reached out his hand for a fist bump, and I obliged. We hadn't been here since the Stanley Cup ended, and I hadn't recalled seeing him anywhere after his alleged couple spat in Camden on July 4th.

"AO, how's it going man?" I asked, sitting down finally.

"Well, my friend, well. I suppose. What're you drinking?"

"Anything wet," I replied, knowing Tammy would be by any moment.

Even after a few seconds, I could tell Adam had sailed through whatever could've been bothering him in the days since he and Megan had their fight. I usually wasn't one for social drama, but in this case, I was interested. Pushing it wasn't the right idea, however, he seemed almost *too* relaxed for someone likely on the outs with his girlfriend.

Tammy came over and took my first order. It wasn't too busy yet, so she felt the liberty to engage in small talk.

"Good to see you guys back again!" she exclaimed.

"Thanks," AO and I both replied cheerfully.

"Billy, I haven't seen Jesse and Hank in a while, have you?"

Hank, Jesse, and I were thick as thieves in high school but had lost steady contact recently, especially this summer. But we were all connected with our roots in Belfast in one way or another. Jesse even dated Tammy's little sister at one point in school.

"No, Jesse's in Orono for the summer at his apartment, and Hank is somewhere near Portland."

"Ah, I see. So then who's this new friend I always see you here with?" she asked inquisitively.

"Adam Olsen," I said. "He went to Camden, but we'll give him a pass."

Adam laughed, and waved to Tammy, introducing himself.

"Nice, welcome," she replied, "I'll get you those beers."

A few minutes later, Tammy came back with another Moose Lager for Adam and a first Allagash for me. Before she walked away, she got the ball rolling between AO and me with just one simple question.

"Hey Billy, sorry to keep being nosy, but I haven't seen Megan LaMarre in a while either, I know you two used to hang out as well."

Adam shot a glance my way, caught somewhere between holding on to the nonchalant attitude he carried and the simmering eagerness to vent about his girlfriend. There was only one way for me to shift the awkwardness from me to him, without casting aspersions about what was going on between Adam and Megan or revealing what I had been up to.

"Ha," I said to Tammy, stammering just slightly. "It's this guy who would know more about Megan. They've been seeing each other for almost a year I think."

From across the table, AO leaned back, almost so far that the buttons on his henley tensed up. He explained to Tammy the usual twenty-something elevator pitch about where Megan was living and what she was doing for work. Tammy nodded and smiled, telling Adam to let her know she said hello. They had been neighbors growing up before the LaMarres moved to Lincolnville.

Now that Tammy had left the second time, I could see Adam's mood shift. He and I were still conversing about the sporting events going on, what we were doing the rest of the summer, and other occasional bar talk, but I could tell that was about to change.

"You know Billy," Adam said, pushing his beer glass away so he could talk with his hands. "I need your help with something."

"Sure, what's that?"

"You've known Megan a long time, right?"

I nodded. Certainly, AO knew by now about the three-week-long romance she shared with me in high school that abruptly ended when Megan transferred to the Magdalene School in Portland.

"Well," he continued. "I think she's mad at me."

I nodded again, waiting for him to continue and hoping it didn't look like I knew that already.

"She doesn't like the way this summer's gone. For some reason, she thinks I'm going to go back to Chamberlain and change my mind about her. Like, I'm gonna dump her or something. It's been since last Christmas that we've been together. Enough time to prove myself, I thought."

"Has anything specific happened to cause an argument?" I asked, again careful with my tone of voice.

"Not really, her parents have never liked me, and that causes rifts sometimes I think."

"I can understand, they certainly come from a different ilk than us."

AO nodded. This was of course true and apparent to us both. While Adam had gone to Camden and then to Chamberlain, and me from Belfast to Dartmouth, neither one of us was born on third base with a silver spoon in our mouths. As I got to know him more personally this summer, I realized my preconceived notions of him being a freeloader and a bullshit artist weren't entirely accurate. More broadly, it was our shared intellect, competitive spirit, and dedication to achievement at a young age that propelled us out of the Midcoast and possibly to a prominent legal or political future.

On the other hand, of course, Megan, for all her talents and likable characteristics, was in many ways still a product of a wealthier class. She could afford a new Bronco with the money she earned because her parents had fronted everything else. This idea must have made Adam clash with the LaMarres, especially when you take into account that they probably weren't pleased with him schlepping their daughter around all summer, typically a season where they routinely jettisoned to places like Bar Harbor or Montauk. However before I could let this go completely, I had to add one more thing to this conversation. Something to end it but also assure that I was simply a bystander.

"Well, man, I wish I had more for you. You're a great guy and I think they'll see that more by the end of the summer."

Deep down, I knew this was partial bullshit. As much as I have grown to appreciate Adam over the last several weeks when we hung out, the fact of the matter was that something still didn't smell right. Sure, he was more genuine than I remembered and had matured, but there was more to the story with him and Megan. And while I needed to understand the dynamics of their relationship for the sake of my plan, I couldn't risk appearing to take any sides. The mission at hand must come first.

***

A midsummer's day in Bayside was an extraordinary thing, especially when the firm gave me a rare off day. Usually, those days began with sunny mornings spent watching the tides and boats come and depart. An afternoon spent with a tee time and a late lunch. An evening spent watching the Sox on television. I couldn't complain, there was no toil on such days. But today, it poured, as it seemingly had for weeks, and was not one of those sunny days. Sam was also expecting me in Belfast at one of our usual meeting spots. Rain or shine.

Soon I found myself driving up the short distance north back to Belfast, rather than my usual south to Camden for work. My windshield wipers went faster than daylight in December but the commute felt slower than a takeout line in Wiscasset. Eventually, I parked on Bridge Street and walked with my arm covering my forehead over to where I met Sam.

Agent Wells stood, cornered against the railing of a pier, not phased by the rain whatsoever. His Helly Hansen rain jacket appeared to be weathering the elements just fine.

"Billy, good to see you – glad you could make it. Figured you would've had to work."

"Rare off day," I replied. "But they have been assigning me more work, so this could be the last for a while. I've already been there six weeks yet the summer is only half over."

"Jeez, throwing ya into the fire, aren't they? Nepotism isn't always a cakewalk, huh?"

"No," I laughed, looking across the river. "It's not."

For a moment, the conversation appeared to be trailing fast. It had been over a month since we began working together and every lead since had come up dry. Our last meeting had ended on a sour note, but I hoped today would be different. And before my gaze even left the tugboat leaving the foggy harbor, my damp thoughts echoed in Sam's voice.

"Well Bakeman, I think we have hit a wall with leads recently," he said, flatly. Rain continued to fall, gathering on his and my shoulders. I nodded.

"Sure has, and you might just want to take it from here anyway. You know, with real law enforcement people." It sounded self-degrading, but in reality, my comment was the truth. Unless I could pry a lead out of Megan's mom and her friend, and without Sam getting the wrong idea about my motives, my contributions in the Conrad Kidd case were irrelevant. I still wanted closure for Myles Jackson, who was already six feet in the ground, and yet I had more work to do for justice. Whether this was worth Sam's time seemed to be in question.

"No, Billy. You've put too much on the line. Your uncle trusts you and you have more legal knowledge at your fingers and you've developed relationships," Sam differed, assuaging my concern for a moment.

"What does my Uncle Jack have to do with this?"

Sam stepped closer, avoiding eye contact with a jogger running along the boardwalk. He sighed.

"You know that stunt I pulled with him and the *Press Herald*?

"How could I forget..."

"Well, it went a little too far. I think he's spooked about your 'family name' and has been digging into our case with the feds and other lawyers."

"So you think he knows that we've met?"

"Not really. But it depends if he or Courtier knows who Conrad Kidd is or what he's up to."

"What do you mean?" I asked.

"If Jack's been poking around with his lawyer friends, he must know what Mitchell's attorney knows - that you went to Kelly Cove before. That guy probably tried to tie your interest to the murder before Atkinson cleared you from foul play and before Mitchell balked."

"Isn't that breaking due process of some kind for people to talk about that?" I interjected.

"Hasn't stopped your girlfriend's mom."

I glared at Sam.

"Well, Jack must have been disappointed when he learned like the rest of us that Jordan Mitchell got nailed easily and surrendered without contest," I proposed.

"Maybe," Sam replied. "Unless he, as a smart attorney, assumed, as we did, that Mitchell wouldn't fall on the sword in court unless he was scared of retribution."

I nodded again.

"And in this case, scared of retribution from someone like Conrad Kidd."

"Well, why don't we pull Jack in, and use his legal resources and connections? He knows a lot about property law and could help with some of that material."

"No, that's what you're for," Sam chuckled.

I shook my head and continued. "He and Doug had a meeting this morning. Why didn't they pull me in if they knew what was going on? I could've helped them."

While only a third-year undergrad, I thought family trust meant something, especially when it involved me directly. Then again, I had lied to them about working with Sam.

"They either didn't tell you because you're too green, they want you to be safe, or," Sam paused and looked me straight in the eye. "Or because they're in a bind."

Eleven

At this point, my Bruins hat was soaked beyond belief, but I stayed persistent, still digesting Sam's thoughts.

"*In a bind?* Now who is the one with wild theories!?" I asked, recalling his reaction to me suggesting my friends were worthy of being called a lead.

"Well, look at the facts Billy. I know Jack's made some calls, supposedly on your behalf. And, I know he's talked to you about the case more than once. Now, I'm aware that he and his partner are taking on a case that seemingly you nor the Sally Fields look-alike at your office are helping with. What am I supposed to conclude?"

I said nothing yet. We sat at a crossroads. We were desperate and this could be a break. I could either walk away now with Wells and eventually every fed he knows aware that I wimped out. Or, I could risk my family's trust in me in pursuit of justice. But you could argue I've done so already.

"Sam," I stated. "I want to help you. I want Conrad Kidd to spend the rest of his life behind bars."

"Good –"

"Let me finish," I interrupted Sam again. We had built enough rapport for him to understand I still respected the hell out of him. "I want to be official. Make me a consultant. No more friendly tips and random meetings. Let's get this done."

"You know what this means right?" Sam asked, before continuing. "We have to get results, and you have to take bigger risks.

Just because you're a consultant and not a criminal informant doesn't mean you won't be burdened with some bad apples. Are you able to agree to that?"

"Yes," I replied. "I know what's right Sam."

Sam peered back at me and nodded.

"So what's our plan?" I added.

"For now, I will work the Mitchell angle. We may have to flush him out to expose anyone, regardless of the sides, including your uncle and Conrad himself."

"What do I do?"

"Sit tight, and be normal. No bullshit. I'd suggest getting closer to that bombshell of yours and figuring out what her mom knows about the court proceedings. If there's evidence there, we'll pursue it."

I nodded and stuck out my hand. The conversation had lasted all of five minutes, but it was worth it. Sam shook my hand and turned around, heading toward downtown and his car.

***

That night, I helped my dad uncover the woodpile after the rain passed for good. Lori was working and therefore missed dinner. Mom made sweet potatoes and steak, a family favorite, and we ate early. Life, for all its complexities, was still simple. In less than two months, I'd spend my nights in a different place. This is where I need to be right now.

However, my bliss was short-lived. I got upstairs about ready to take a shower when I noticed a text from Megan, thirty minutes old.

Hey Billy. Adam is in Augusta tonight for roller
hockey. Wanna hang out?

This DEA consultant business was way too easy. I replied to the text.

Sure! Where do you want to meet?

My house? 7? We can get ice cream at the Beach.

Great – I'll see you soon.

The whole drive down to Lincolnville, I couldn't help smiling. This was what a former infielder like me would call a triple play. Hanging out with Megan, despite what I led on, was still something to look forward to. Then of course there was ice cream. Lastly, though, was the case at hand. *It was Sam's orders*, after all.

When I pulled into her driveway, I remembered the night of the party when I first learned of Jordan Mitchell. There has been a lot of water under the bridge since then. I'm surprised she didn't ask to hang out in Belfast or Camden, but perhaps she was conscious of people getting the wrong idea, no matter how angry she was with Adam.

She emerged from the house, wearing gym shorts and the same UMaine tee from our first encounter this summer. The same sunglasses stood on her forehead too, completing the look. She offered to drive, but I told her no, saying it would be too painful to just sit in a Bronco without driving it. Megan told me it was her dad's orders. I obliged and drove us the short distance up the coast.

The sun was just beginning to go down, and we headed toward the beach, where a small strip of business began with a hotel and ended with a post office. In between lay an ice cream stand, which would probably close at eight or nine. Across the street from there was the parking lot of a lobster shack, where we had last seen one another a week before. When we got out of the car, she looked over at me, pushing the brown hair out of her face, a result of the sea breeze.

"This would've been fun to do last week, instead of me waiting over there."

"True," I said, agreeing.

"Surprisingly, I'm not sick of ice cream yet."

I was confused at first, then realized she did work at a place like this.

"Right, and this time, you don't have to run back to work."

She laughed.

We sat at a picnic table in a grassy spot, near a shit ton of tiger lilies and bees. That wasn't a bother. She told stories about her past vacations and dreamed of future ones. She asked who I thought the Sox would trade for later this month, understanding the moment and what I may be interested in talking about. Before we knew it, an hour had passed, and the sun started to set completely. Occasionally, she would peer off toward the bay and spin her Stanley in her hands, only to look back at me and come up with a different topic. From my eyes, it felt like Megan LaMarre was feeling free again. Free from her parents who expected her to be the next Clara Barton. Free from Adam, whose lack of punctuality and attendance drove her crazy. More significantly, free from the stress that would cause most college kids like us to waste our summers feeling uptight about the future. Or in my case, stressed about justice for a veteran-turned-substitute teacher-turned murder victim.

The sun finally disappeared behind the gold horizon. I reached for my keys on the table, realizing that this outing was nearing its end, without even a mention of the case.

"We're leaving already?" Megan inquired.

"Yeah," I chuckled, pointing to the employee nearby, taking down the open flag. "This place is about to close."

Megan sighed, and got up, heading for the sidewalk and the Jeep. But before I could get to the other side of the vehicle, she called out my name.

"Billy," she said. "Let's not go back yet."

I'd heard that tone of hers before, years before when we left school during study hall and spent all of that period and lunchtime downtown getting pizza and people-watching. Her adventurous spirit is still unparalleled today, unchanged despite the changes in our own lives.

I laughed and told her I had nowhere to be, realizing it wasn't a bad thing to prolong this evening. Megan got into the Jeep and turned the radio dial to a pop station.

Once driving, she directed me to a freshwater beach up the way at a nearby lake, while telling broken stories about stuff she had seen online or remembered from when we were younger. I wondered if these were things that she missed talking about, and that Adam didn't understand. He was very analytical at times like I was, but perhaps they didn't have the history or the willingness to engage in small talk like we were now.

If Megan liked a song she turned it up and if she didn't, she changed the station - almost too much considering that not one song played all the way through by the time we reached the second beach in a few minutes. This one was more secluded than the oceanfront spot we were just at, similar to Kelly Cove. However, unlike the place where I found Myles, it was less ominous after dark and had freshwater rather than saltwater, creating a more aesthetically welcoming environment. Its waters were placid and the sound of frogs and loons lingered in the background. We continued talking over them, skipping rocks, and reminiscing about things passed by, as we had done all evening.

The moment broke when she brought up the night when we first learned that Jordan Mitchell was a person of interest.

"Remember the night we played truth or dare at my house?" she asked.

"Yes," I chuckled again, "I remember jumping in your pool."

"Well - what if we played right now, and picked up where we left off?"

The last question that night was about Myles and who killed him. I was game if it meant more information and more time here with her. I nodded.

"Okay," I said. "Who's going first?"

"I know you're gonna pick 'truth', so let me do a dare for you first."

Seemed like a fair deal. "Alright, then."

"So, this is gonna be a bargain. You do my dare, I do your truth, and so on."

"Yeah, that's how the game works," I replied. She smirked.

"I dare you to jump in the lake," Megan declared. "It's good luck. Last time you jumped in my pool you had a breakthrough – and something tells me you are still looking into that stuff."

I laughed, "Now who's the lawyer," I said. "Let me counter: If you jump in, I'll jump in, and then we'll stick to truths from then on."

Megan sighed. "Fine."

My finger pointed directly toward the lake, where a rock pile was formed. but she hustled the other way down the shoreline behind me, disappearing into the dark. Against better judgment, I decided to follow, eventually hearing splashes in a shallower part of the lake. I slid my sandals and my polo shirt off and set them on a fallen tree. My shorts were twill, but I kept them on, surrendering that they wouldn't dry on their own tonight. On my way into the cold lake, I saw her tee shirt, shorts, sports bra, socks, and sneakers bundled out in a heap on a flat rock. In the distance, I noticed her silhouette and she called out for me. Swimming after dark alongside a now topless former flame of mine was not on today's agenda, but alas, here we were. I eventually got up to shoulder level, thank God. She swam closer, water up to her neck, and I couldn't help but give her a hard time for this.

"I thought we were jumping in?!"

Megan shook her head, "You changed the rules and so did I."

"Well, last time I had swim trunks. This is different."

"You'll live," she croaked, noticeably treading water. "In fact," Megan breathed, "I'll even go first since I already messed up our sequence."

"Sure," I stammered, realizing it was only getting colder.

Megan paused and retreated a few feet, the waxing moon illuminating her shoulders. Her wet hair was draped over them. Then she smiled.

"What have you *really been doing* this summer?"

"Seems a little open-ended for a truth," I replied. "I've just been working a lot."

"Nope, I don't buy it," Megan contradicted. Then she treaded a few yards to my right. "I think you're either hanging out with us because you like me or because you want to know what I know about the Jackson murder."

"Well," I raised my voice playfully. "You're the one who brought me out here half-naked into this lake – why don't you just tell me what you know and we can go get dry."

Megan smiled. "See, I knew you were still interested in this. I can tell by the way you've been acting."

"Yeah, yeah, yeah," I said. "You got me, I'm still interested. What's up?"

Megan swam to her right, back into the moonlight.

"Apparently, there's not a sentencing date yet for Jordan, even though he pleaded guilty."

"So you think the state has reservations about putting him away too soon?"

Megan tried to shrug. "You're the future attorney, what do you think?"

"It's possible," I said. "But only if they think Mitchell could still be innocent. That's a big ask though. Usually, they just want to put somebody away to assure the public that it's over."

"Makes sense," Megan said. "Especially 'cause Tracy Jackson is lawyering up. I think she wants to protect herself from retribution in case the affair gets out. I still can't believe nobody knows about –"

"Wait," I interrupted. "She's lawyering up?"

"I dunno. My dad just said he saw her talking to some attorney in Camden. Doug something... middle-aged guy."

I froze. It could be Doug Courtier, which explains his weird behavior earlier this week.

"Damn, she might be meeting with my uncle's partner."

"Well there you go," Megan replied. "You can figure it out now."

She laughed and splashed water on my face.

"We can continue once we're dry," she continued. "With non-legalese questions."

I laughed nervously and watched her swim back into the darkness, toward the shore. As the water got shallower, I followed. She turned so her back was to me and reached for her bra and her shirt. I leaned back and looked to my left, giving her privacy while she finished changing.

Then I made my way to shore, trying to avoid getting any colder. My Jeep had a spare clean towel I used in case it rained. It was never intended for a late-night swim, but I lent it to Megan to use, telling her I'd drip dry and get over it.

We got back near the Jeep, and Megan leaned on the driver's side door with the windows still open. She looked up at the moonlight and waited for me to get closer. My mind was still focused on Doug's possible connection to the Jacksons, and what that meant for Sam and me. However, it was difficult not to notice the way Megan felt comfortable tonight. Many other times this summer she had been hamstrung by frustration, such as the night we saw each other at the lobster shack or apparently on the Fourth with Adam.

She glanced over at me as I started to get my keys ready, and I outstretched my hand, indicating I changed my mind and wanted a turn with the towel. Our eyes met again, and she thanked me for obliging her spontaneous wishes. I went to take the towel but she held on the other end, allowing us both to drift closer. She tossed the towel through the open window and I let my tee shirt leave my hands.

Instantly, our lips met for the first time in four years, once again behind a car. Her hands moved up my body to my shoulders, and mine stayed at her waist, her skin was still wet. We stayed like that for what felt like a minute before breaking away. Megan smiled and we returned to the Jeep. I picked up my tee shirt and followed. Afterward, I opened my mouth when I probably shouldn't have.

"It's a shame things didn't work out between us back then," I said.

Megan smiled again. "Yeah," she replied. "It is." Then she looked back out the window and slid down to put her feet up on the dashboard. Finally, a few seconds later, she continued, "It was the best three weeks of your life, though."

I rotated to look at her, my turn signal on even though the road was empty. We both laughed.

Twelve

A couple of days later, I accompanied Sam on a visit to see Tracy Jackson. Nobody in my family was home so nobody knew I was gone when Sam picked me up along Bluff Road. Tracy lived a mile or so away from us in a modern house that Myles built, on Tall Oaks Drive, a stone's throw from where I went to elementary school. Years before, I remember seeing Myles outside there working on a shed, and realizing that's where he lived, only a couple weeks after having him as a substitute teacher for the first time in science class. Soon after, Marty learned of the Jacksons' boat repair shop when doing taxes for a local family. Then another time, Tracy was Lori's nurse when she had her appendix removed. Helen was, of course, familiar with the Jacksons via the high school. All of this created an environment in which I weirdly felt both comfortable and uncomfortable at this house given the circumstances. I could only imagine how Tracy would react when I appeared alongside a fed. Sam believed my presence would calm Tracy, and make her realize that a near-family friend like myself wouldn't do anything to jeopardize the situation.

Upon entering the driveway, I saw the same shed that Myles had built years before. It was worn by now, and the midsummer grass had grown around it, weeks since the last volunteer had probably mowed. I wondered who was helping Tracy out with Jordan awaiting jail and Myles dead. We approached the door and Sam led, knocking four loud times with his badge already in hand.

Tracy answered the door, alarmed at first but surprisingly eased when she saw me standing nearby. All along, Tracy knew I was the one to find her husband only a few additional miles away.

"Hello ma'am, my name is Sa –"

"Why did you bring Billy here?" Tracy interrupted. "Is he in trouble?"

She and I made eye contact. Her navy blue tee shirt had flour stains on it, a sign that we interrupted her cooking. Her blond hair was well-kept, but she had bags under her eyes, a sign that she may have worked late the night before.

"Yes," I said. "I'm fine."

"Mrs. Jackson, my name is Sam Wells, I'm with the Drug Enforcement Administration."

Tracy looked confused, but then her eyes narrowed again, and she nodded. A good sign.

"Billy and I have something we'd like to talk to you about."

"What's that?"

"Your husband," Sam replied, his voice shaking slightly.

She looked at me, and I nodded, so she let us in.

Tracy led us to the living room and she sat down abruptly and quickly, glancing over at the kitchen mess she had left.

"What's going on?" she asked finally.

Sam began, first telling the story of how he wanted to use my knowledge of the area, Myles' disappearance, and his discovery to conclude who was really behind the murder of her husband. Tracy obliged, but stated she had told investigators all that she knew. Wells was visibly skeptical and explained that he had reason to believe that Myles was going to reveal information to authorities about a statewide drug cartel. Tracy shook her head and sighed. The room was quiet for a second before she spoke up again. As Tracy began talking, she pointed at me.

"Billy found Myles dead. And that man from the auto shop – Jordan – turned himself in already. Your information is wrong, there's no leverage there."

Sam sat there and looked at me first. Then he looked back at Tracy.

"With all due respect, Mrs. Jackson, they didn't need to keep your husband for leverage. They had you."

I cringed.

"Who the hell do you think you're talking to, agent?" Tracy muttered.

I had to step in.

"Tracy, I think what Sam is trying to say is..."

"Billy," Tracy cut in, looking me in the eye. "I know what he is trying to say."

We both paused and waited for her to keep speaking. It felt like five minutes had passed before Tracy finally spoke up again.

"You think I'm dumb, guys? I know what you want me to say. I know half the town thinks I was sleeping with Jordan Mitchell."

Sam and I looked at each other again, shocked.

"Well, I'm not here to talk about your personal life, Mrs. Jackson."

"Bullshit you're not," Tracy said.

More silence.

"Yes, I slept with him, but that's not important." The defensiveness in her voice was paramount. She *did* know that it was important, so important she acted like she didn't know Jordan Mitchell minutes before.

"Actually it is," Sam replied. "I believe your relationship to both men is the lynchpin to the whole drug investigation."

Tracy glanced over at the kitchen stove clock and then back at us. Her sternness wore off and she began to tear up. Her rough personality was a front, and it was clear this woman was still hurting. She quickly broke down, now explaining that the rumors were true without much of a fight. Tracy had been in an extra-marital affair with Jordan Mitchell for almost eighteen months. They met at the hospital when Jordan brought Mrs. Percival there for an x-ray and they began seeing each other in the days and weeks after. Soon, it had become an elaborate scheme and was convenient during the summer months when Myles worked long hours at the repair shop. We sat on the sofa and continued to listen as Tracy insisted that Myles didn't lay a finger on Jordan before the murder occurred, but Sam pushed back immediately.

"Ma'am, we're not concerned about the affair explicitly, no civil or criminal law was broken with that."

Tracy responded, "So, if not, what is the focus here, and why bring a kid into this? Billy did not have anything to do with what Jordan Mitchell did to Myles and he is certainly not in a drug cartel."

"Thank you, Tracy," I said. "But Sam and I believe that not only did the cartel kill Myles, but that they framed Jordan for his murder."

At that moment, Tracy's demeanor changed drastically, as if she heard an answer to prayer, her own *Deus ex machina* - God from a machine. The front which echoed the public story vanished. I wondered if she was waiting for somebody official to acknowledge what we all knew to be true. Surely I knew now that it wasn't her fault that this had all happened.

She perked up and breathed heavily before turning to Sam. Temporary relief, then fear presented itself over her entire body.

"Mr. Wells, you're right," she trembled. "Something strange was going on with my husband."

We looked on with intent, and Sam insisted she continue. Tracy corroborated Sam's story that Myles was at odds with a group of dangerous men but insisted she didn't know who or why. The day before I found him dead, Tracy told Myles that she had to work late for the holiday weekend, but in reality, she planned on running away with Jordan to Cape Cod. "A dismal idea, in retrospect," she told us. Later that day, when Jordan never showed up for their getaway, Tracy was confused. She sought him out at the Percival house, where they presumably reconciled and spent the night together in a guest room, but never left Bayside. This matched what Megan had told us at her party weeks earlier, so clearly her mom's friend had legitimate information. The next morning, Tracy returned home with guilt, expecting to see Myles. But he had vanished. Initially, Tracy believed he had caught onto her affair and left. As the day drew on, she became concerned and called the police.

After I found the body, and Myles was immediately declared dead, things got tricky for Tracy in a hurry. Jordan soon became a person of interest after the discovery of the stolen truck and the handgun, and he surrendered to the police. That part we all knew, but my burning question all along was why Tracy didn't give Jordan up immediately if he actually killed Myles, or conversely, why she didn't protect his potential alibi by revealing their affair.

Tracy explained how she believed the same people who were after Myles must have been the ones to murder him. But if Tracy also thought Jordan was innocent, she certainly did nothing to help prove it. In fact, at the time of Myles' death, law enforcement officers were impatient with Tracy's lack of direction. However, Tracy told us she had never met any of those men before. At this point in the conversation, knowing that he was onto a bigger story that could involve Conrad Kidd, Sam interrupted.

"Alright, so it seems like we're on the same page, but why didn't you come clean and expose your affair? Wouldn't that have helped authorities rule out Jordan as the primary murder suspect? If you spent the night together, you're a key witness to his whereabouts."

"That's just not gonna happen," Tracy said, shaking her head. "If the public knows we were involved, they'll think Jordy wanted to kill my husband. Deep down every jury will have that bias."

"I don't think so," I interrupted. "You already said people suggest that to be true already. Hell, we knew about the affair weeks ago but we didn't believe Mitchell did it... So if it's revealed that you were with him, you'll put pressure back on the authorities."

"Well, then I would be openly admitting that I withheld information during the investigation."

"Don't worry about that," Sam said. "I can take care of it."

Tracy still seemed hesitant, so I chimed in again, almost serving as if I were her attorney.

"And let's put pressure on the mechanic too," I said. "If the public knows Jordan has a solid alibi, then the guy from the auto shop can also help us. I don't think he gave the cops a statement beyond the missing truck, and there aren't sufficient cameras at his place. We'll have to get to him first though, because whoever was after Myles will want to cover their tracks."

Sam nodded, but Tracy was still hesitant. Her mood had gone from stern to panicked to relieved to ambiguous. She was impossible to read.

Finally, she spoke up. "That won't be possible. The mechanic left for Florida indefinitely according to his associates. Hasn't shown up since. His business is dormant."

"Is he missing too?" Sam asked.

"Don't know. That's just what I was told initially by Jordan. Maybe he got spooked by the break-in and bailed. It didn't matter, Jordan gave up."

"But you have no idea who these bad guys are, and you've never met them?" I asked.

"Nope. Not a clue," Tracy replied, shaking her head. "But Jordan is in jail because of them."

"So if you *truly* think Jordan is innocent too, just help us regardless," Sam insisted. "We can bring justice to Myles, and we can clear everyone's name."

"Okay," Tracy sighed. "Fine. But I want a statement drafted and I want a new lawyer present when I talk to law enforcement."

I perked up. Sam looked over as if to tell me to sit back down.

"Alright, Mrs. Jackson. We thank you a lot for your cooperation. Do you know who will be representing you?"

My throat stung. I hadn't yet told Sam that she was supposedly talking to my uncle's partner. Further, Sam didn't know that the sentencing date was being stalled. Again, whoever Megan's mother was talking to knew her shit.

"Doug Courtier in Camden, I want him. He knows the Percivals and will help me."

"Okay, thanks ma'am," Sam replied. He shot me a look. We both got up and Tracy leaned into me for a hug. It was the most confusing fifteen minutes of my life.

Sam and I returned to the car, and he began backing out of her driveway. We continued down Tall Oaks until we met the main road.

"I'd drop you off at home, Billy, but I wouldn't want you to have to explain that. Can you walk from here?"

"Yes," I said.

"Good, I'm headed to Camden."

"What for?" I asked.

"To talk to Dougie-boy."

***

Later that afternoon, I decided to drop by my favorite hot dog stand in Belfast for lunch. Since I was a kid, it was one of my favorite places to eat. Fair prices, well-cooked food, and easy access made it a favorite for others too, even year-round. Locals like me knew not to go between 11:30 and 1 unless you wanted to wait in line. That's how good it was.

When I approached the ordering window, I saw a donation jar for the Jacksons. I'm sure by now expenses were beginning to add up. The stand didn't take credit cards, so it was a smart place to put one of those. My order only came to $7.50, so the remaining $2.50 I had from breaking a ten-dollar bill went in there. Considering the rigamarole we put Tracy through this morning, it was the best I could do at the moment.

The next morning I returned to work at the firm. We were just finishing up an eminent domain case and the paperwork was seemingly endless. Toward the middle of the day and lunch, Doug swung by the desk to sign and look over some of the documents I had prepared. His demeanor was normal, and part of me wondered if my assumptions were way off. There could be another Doug in Camden who practiced law and specialized in criminal defense or something more related. Perhaps Sam hadn't talked to him yet.

"Great job, Billy. I'll need these for Friday and now we won't have to make too many adjustments." Doug seemed proud of my work.

"Awesome, that's a relief," I laughed.

Doug patted me on the back and headed for the door. "I won't be back today, Billy - so remind your uncle if he forgot again."

We both laughed.

An hour or so later, after I had worked through lunch starting a new case on subdividing, Jack traipsed through the doorway carrying brown paper bags and glass bottles of Coke. Miss B looked up, shook her head, and continued putting on her rain jacket. The rain hadn't let up all morning, and her lunch departure would probably be short-lived. Jack called over to me and asked for me to join him.

"Pretty soon Billy, you're gonna outshine me as the hardest-working Bakeman. Come on in here and take a load off!"

We sat down in his office and Uncle Jack began to slide a Coke bottle my way, only to pull it back and grab a Modelo from the fridge behind his desk. He outstretched his hand.

"Don't tell Miss B or your mother."

I laughed. "They both suspect already."

Jack smiled and pulled out a Subway sandwich, handing me the second one. "I hope you don't mind," he said.

We started talking, mostly about whether the Pats' rookie quarterback would see any action this year beyond the preseason. Uncle Jack was the quarterback at Andrews College in Lewiston for all four years, passing for twenty-eight touchdowns and running for seven during his senior campaign, enough to make him first-team all-conference and a member of the school's Hall of Fame. At Belfast High, Jack won a state championship as a junior starting QB with my dad as the upstart freshman tailback. Chief Milton was a linebacker and went on to play at Maine Maritime Academy before joining the Coast Guard Reserves and then the Belfast P.D. Growing up around these men, I had learned my share of football strategy, even though I was the black sheep and preferred hockey and baseball.

"Well, if he gets the play in on time I think he'll be able to make adjustments at the line of scrimmage regardless," I added.

"That's true. Hey, speaking of being on time, Billy. I noticed you've been getting your work done efficiently, even though you've been off a couple of days this week."

I nodded.

"Is there any reason why you can't start the longer schedule tomorrow instead of Monday? We'd love to get through this rush of cases sooner and without having to hire a paralegal."

"Of course," I said. It was only an extra two days of longer hours anyway.

"Great, thanks, Billy. Like we said on Monday, it's been great having you here but we'd love to have *more of your focus.*"

The last four words of that sentence sounded like a perfect storm. Unlike Sam, I didn't suspect that Jack knew what we were up to. He probably just thought I was spending too much time fogged up somewhere on a dead-end road with Megan LaMarre. Either way, this new schedule was going to make it harder to see Sam and nail Conrad Kidd for everything he was worth.

Thirteen

The next day, Sam met me at the Dairy Queen drive-thru. We debriefed the visit with Tracy Jackson and I informed him of my new demands at the firm. He wasn't pleased, but he understood. It gave him a reason to bring up whether or not he had met Doug yesterday. But before I could admit to Sam that I had learned about Doug and Tracy working together first from Megan, he broke the short silence with a whopper of his own.

"Billy, I spoke to Doug yesterday night and you're not going to like what he told me."

I gulped, hoping it wasn't something that implicated the LaMarres in all of this.

"He did meet with Tracy already," Sam began. "And, he has been the Percival family's lawyer for a few years now. That's why he has a Jordan Mitchell connection. He assured me that he's clean though and I believe him."

"Okay, so what's the bad news?" I asked.

Sam sighed. "Doug got ahold of the police report, and so has your uncle."

"How?!" I exclaimed.

"Two reasons. For starters, Atkinson, Lopez, Milton, and Jack are all well-connected 'round here. Everyone was thorough but everyone kept their secrets until now. Favors never end. Second, your uncle is family, and he apparently got you to sign something saying he was your attorney."

I thought back to the stipend increase I recently signed. Classic Uncle Jack to put it in there. A rookie move on my part to fall for it.

"Alright, well shit," I said flatly.

"Yeah, now he can pretty much take you away from us at any time and we have to oblige."

"So what else is there to know though? That I was pok-"

"That you've been hired as a consultant."

My head dropped. "Alright, we could just tell Jack I'm done with you."

"You aren't gonna want to do that," Sam piped. "He doesn't know about you and me yet anyway."

A sigh of relief came over me, but I was still uneasy.

"How come?" I asked.

"Well, for starters, Doug was pretty adamant about you and me keeping an eye on Tracy and Jordan. He's unsure of their story."

"Okay, whatever. I don't get why Doug is getting involved here."

Sam sighed again. "He's just trying to save his own ass over there at the firm."

"What do you mean?"

"Look. Jack knows you weren't really fishing that night. But even worse, according to Doug, your uncle is indeed friendly with Conrad Kidd and therefore knows why it's taking this long to put Mitchell away, so they're both getting squirrely about the whole thing."

"Are you kidding me?" I shouted.

"Quiet down Billy – No, I'm not."

Sam explained how Doug learned of Jack's relationship with Conrad Kidd earlier this week. Doug began to raise questions about Jordan Mitchell's assumed guilt and other legal minds were beginning to wonder why no sentencing date had been made. Doug suspected something was up when suddenly every new case at the firm was on his desk and not Jack's. Apparently during a separate benign private conversation about the upcoming Mitchell trial, Jack let his mouth go and that's when the admission slipped. Jack confided in Doug and confessed to helping the cartel evade law enforcement through his relationships in the region.

Early on, Jack insisted to the cartel on not being involved with the murder of Myles Jackson but knew about it soon after it was planned, and did nothing to stop it. Jack's role was primarily to help get permits so the cartel could commandeer the land and vessels needed for smuggling operations. He would also leverage his friendships with the police, Coasties, harbormasters, and local businessmen to tip off Kidd's men if problems arose. In one instance, Jack was asked to map the possible whereabouts of every fishing vessel, every cutter, and every small craft in the Bay before an op. It wouldn't have been difficult for my uncle, who was a skilled recreational cartographer and studied oceanography alongside law. The contraband from that mission subsequently made it to Saint John unscathed and untracked. Sam recalled hearing of that operation.

At first, Doug simply encouraged Jack to get out if he could, fearful of the ramifications if he were caught or if he crossed the cartel. Jack wanted to but said he was in too deep, noting that he didn't want to end up like Myles. That's when Doug decided to enlist the help of Tracy Jackson in proving Jordan Mitchell's innocence. Doug was on our side, but I was speechless - so much so that I didn't even bother telling Sam about Megan's story.

"I understand if this is a lot to take. I'm floored too, to be honest," Sam concluded.

Meanwhile, I was overcome with feelings of betrayal. My uncle, in bed with a cartel and using me to cover his own ass. More loyalty to the law had come from a dude I met weeks ago than from my own family.

"So what am I supposed to do now? I can't go back to work there knowing all of this. Does Doug know about you and me?"

"Yes, he does," Sam replied. "And you guys are gonna help me bring Jack in."

I almost threw up.

"And how is this going to happen?" I croaked.

Sam pulled out a piece of metal the size of a dime.

"We're gonna bug his office."

***

On the morning of July 23rd, I woke up at 7 AM and met Sam in the parking lot of the Ferry terminal at Lincolnville Beach. It had been seven days since Megan and I shared our escapades in Lincolnville, but this time it was all business. The parking lot was full of commuters to Islesboro, the nearby island, which allowed us to blend into a crowd. Shortly, I would meet Maya Putnam, Sam's supervisor from Boston, who would oversee the op. She had received a warrant to bug Jack's office based on both Doug's testimony and other obtained communication records. The plan was for me to arrive at work earlier than usual and for Doug to arrive at the same time and keep a lookout for my uncle or Miss B. Then, I would plant the bug and we'd return to normal business. If we were caught, Putnam and Sam would be on standby. The goal would be to hear anything that would indicate the whereabouts and machinations of Kidd or his henchmen.

Minutes later, Putnam arrived and met us at Sam's car for final details. She looked like a badass and was supposedly a former Boston P.D. lieutenant. Her idea of retirement evidently included knocking down doors of drug dealers from Barnstable to Bangor instead of finding a quiet beach in Bermuda. Putnam was the one who signed off on me being a consultant, so I owed her nothing but respect. The final detail in the plan was to clear out the office at lunchtime to see if Jack made any calls while he was alone. We wanted to provide enough suspicion for Jack to make a move, but not too much to risk tipping him off.

It began without a hunch. Putnam and Sam wore plain clothes and staked out at Ford & Breen with coffee. Meanwhile, Doug stayed near the door while I put the bug on the inside of Jack's football helmet from college, which was prominently displayed underneath his hanging jersey and below the diplomas. Suddenly, Doug motioned me out of his office frantically. I began to move but not before Jack and Miss B entered through the main door together. Doug on lookout duty was like the Atlanta Falcons in the Super Bowl.

"Why are you here so early?!" Jack asked us.

"We could say the same to you," Doug replied, shooting him a look.

"Oh you know, hair appointment for me later," Miss B. retorted. "Needed to make up for some time."

Jack said nothing of why he was early. Instead, he looked over at me. "Billy, what were you doing in my office?"

"Oh, uh just checking out your memorabilia. We were talking about Doug's time playing golf at Trinity. Nothing compared to football at Andrews, am I right?"

Now Doug shot me a look.

"You're right, nothing compared to the gridiron," Jack solidified. He walked toward me and brushed his hand over his helmet and a trophy. "Some people think I should keep this stuff at home, but you never saw the guy from *Suits* leave his Michael Jordan balls anywhere else but the office." Jack turned to me, his hand dangerously close to the football helmet. "What do you say we get started, guys?"

We all retreated to our desks. He definitely suspected something, but I couldn't know yet if he was onto all of us.

***

By lunchtime, we knew Miss B was going to go get a sandwich at the Deli. We timed that with a "client visit" in which Doug would pretend to take me out to work on a case. Miraculously, that worked out well meaning Jack would be alone at his office for some time. We hoped he would make a move. Sam and Maya were listening in on the bug and knew it had been set. If either amounted to anything, we would find out at some point, but probably not immediately.

Doug and I drove to the courthouse and back, then did a few laps around town in his Land Cruiser until about ninety minutes had passed. When we returned to the firm, we were stunned to see Miss B and Jack practically tethered to their desks with Maya and Sam standing there waiting for us.

I wasn't sure if I was supposed to act like I knew them or not, this was not discussed at all ahead of time.

"Who the hell are you guys?" I croaked.

"You can cut the shit, Billy," Uncle Jack hissed.

"Ole Jackie here decided to make a phone call while you were gone. He walked right into our trap," Sam said, making a circle with his fingers and pacing around the office.

Doug scratched the back of his head and looked over at me. Sam continued.

"And, Brooke Shields over here," Sam pointed to Miss B. "We discovered she's been getting a little chatty at the salon. The appointment today has been canceled."

Sam could be a real prick if he needed to be, which is why he made a great DEA agent. He explained to us that Miss B would be cooperating in exchange for her wrongdoing which included covering for Jack and leaking information to people like Megan's mother. Maya then cut in to describe the phone call from Jack to a cartel source that focused on "cleaning things up" now that "his kin was involved." He was also on tape admitting to "bailing their asses out."

I stood there, once again in shock. Amazingly, Sam and Maya had concocted this plan enough to surprise even Doug and me. Maya stood up, her badge firmly clipped to her tight black shirt. She reached for her handcuffs, and arrested my uncle, stating the allegations of conspiracy and accessory, and then reading him his Miranda rights.

Putnam led him out, but not before Jack turned to me and said, "Nice audible, Billy."

I watched him march out the door as he had many times before, but now in handcuffs and with a return date unknown.

***

By some miracle, I spent the rest of the day with Doug at the firm, finishing what we could for work and making the whole situation as normal as possible for our current clients. Sam stayed too, along with the district attorney Marcus Jefferson and Miss B, to go over the next steps and the ensuing court procedures. Putnam was long gone, probably on her way to another sting operation by then. I couldn't focus. Finally, at 3:46, Doug told me I could leave and to come back tomorrow to help him with the inevitable dissolution of the firm. Without Jack's side of the partnership, Bakeman & Courtier couldn't survive. And yet, it would be the youngest and most unqualified of the Bakeman men to help the only Courtier see that reality through.

***

At 4:09, I sent my Jeep into the driveway, hoping to get home quickly before Marty. I had no idea where Lori and Helen were but I needed to get my story straight. Mom could be anywhere at this time during the summer, especially on Farmer's Market days. However, instead of finding the driveway empty, Dad's truck sat parallel to the shelter we erected for the new lawnmower. He had beaten me home. I parked next to him and made a beeline for the door, but before I knew it Marty emerged from the house and onto the porch.

I saw my father's dim look.

"Sit down, son," he said gently. I joined him on the deck chairs, sitting face to face on the long flat sections.

"I just got off the phone with Aunt Bonny," he continued. "She tells me Uncle Jack has been arrested in connection with a drug bust."

I nodded. "Yes, I know."

"She also tells me that you were involved..." Dad trailed off. "As a consultant."

My dad was a smart man. Maybe not a lawyer like his older brother, but certainly someone who was used to being taken less seriously than he should be, and I was a lot like him in many ways. His tone was not that of disappointment in me, but rather of anger toward Jack for letting me get too close, or perhaps embarrassment on his part for not seeing what I was doing.

I explained to him how I was approached because of the link between this case and Myles' death. However, I also explained how this is very fluid and that we'd be in danger if the cartel knew how much any of us had learned over the last few weeks, including about Uncle Jack. Finally, he cut me off and told me I didn't have to say any more tonight. Our family would need time to process this new reality. Chief Milton, also shaken by the betrayal, assured Dad he would personally protect us if it came to that. Dad began to walk toward the door but turned back to me.

"So Billy, what time do you have to be there tomorrow, to you know, help clean this up?"

"Courtier said ten o'clock."

"Alright, how about I make a tee time for 7:30 and we'll play a quick nine – not too early?"

"No, sir," I laughed.

Marty shot a quick smile, enough to infer that we were both temporarily cheered up in what was an impossible situation. Despite all the drama of the last eight weeks, Dad knew just what we needed.

Fourteen

Marty Bakeman absolutely tattooed his drive on the fourth hole, and he left his Titleist driver cocked in a follow-through as he watched the ball soar down the fairway.

"That'll do," he chuckled before leaving the tee box and inviting my turn. We both knew it would be difficult to match that shot.

But as I stepped up to the tee with my Paradym firmly gripped, I noticed a familiar figure lurking in the distance near the fifth box. It was Adam Olsen, joined by Tim, the smart guy from Chamberlain who was at the party weeks before. I realized I hadn't seen Adam or Megan in a while. After all, it had been almost two weeks since he and I had beers at Gillie's and exactly a week since Megan and I made out at the pond. Considering AO hadn't threatened to beat me with a golf club yet, I suppose he didn't know about our late-night swimming adventure.

Despite his ignorance of the situation, it wouldn't hurt to unload the driver here while he was watching, outdo my dad's tee shot, and impress everyone. I regained my focus and began my swing, sending the ball flying deep into the sky far past my dad's ball and only a few dozen yards shy of the pin. My dad hooted, and I could even see Adam and Tim clap in the distance.

At the end of the round, Dad offered to take the cart back and I went into the clubhouse to fill my water bottle. Adam and Tim were leaving and they saw me, congratulating me on that great shot. We exchanged pleasantries, and I approached the fountain. After filling my Yeti high, I noticed another one had been left behind. It was black with a thick handle, covered only by a Sugarloaf sticker and another one which read: *McGARY for SENATE.*

I raced outside to try and catch Adam before he left, but I was too late. Instead, I met Marty at the car and we made the short drive home. I could return the tumbler to Adam at another time.

***

As much as a great round of golf cleared my head, the drive to Camden from Bayside made it gray all over again. The goal at the firm was to somehow help me get the remaining required hours for my internship. Later, Sam and Jefferson would come by and we'd see about my future involvement as a consultant. In all likelihood, the ongoing drug trafficking investigation into Conrad Kidd's cartel would fall into the lap of Sam and also Patricia Marvin, the assistant U.S. attorney from Portland. Meanwhile, anything to do with the Jacksons and their newfound loose ends would be the responsibility of Jefferson, Roger Atkinson, and the police. Should they intersect, Sam, Putnam, Marvin, and Jefferson would figure that out on their own. My role as a consultant was probably going to end today effectively, and all I had to show for it all was an uncle awaiting arraignment and more questions than answers.

When I walked into the office, Miss Browning's desk was empty and vacant. Jack's office was being searched by what looked like FBI agents. I was ushered into the side room by Doug, who had just finished talking to some of the agents and was trying to keep the shades closed so nobody from outside looked in the windows. I hadn't yet seen the news or been on my phone much today, but it was clear the authorities were treading carefully with all the rumors swirling and suspects still at large.

"I'm so sorry, Billy," Doug said, reaching for my shoulder.

"Thanks, Doug," I replied. "You don't have to say more."

In many respects, my work this summer had made me closer to Doug than my uncle, even before all of this fell into our lives at the firm. He trusted me and I trusted him. Much of the same sentiment was shared with Sam, who picked me out of a crop to help him solve a career-defining case. I wondered if any of that would matter beyond today.

"Look, Billy, I'm not going to see this through here," Doug continued.

He pointed to a sign on the wall. "Bakeman" had already been removed, and Doug's last name would be coming down too. Word would soon get out that we were underwater.

"I see, so what are you going to do?" I asked.

"Tomorrow, I leave for Pennsylvania. I have a cousin in Harrisburg who does work like ours and I'll be seeing if I fit in there. Meanwhile, I am getting our clients transferred to Johnson, Ricker, & Levesque. There aren't going to be many folks left now that Jack is going to be disbarred. Those who have already found out all jumped ship overnight."

A look of sadness filled his face. Certainly, it was bad if Uncle Jack wasn't fighting for preservation or if they had liquidated all of our assets and clients to our chief competition.

"In fact," Doug continued. "I've already called Shirley Levesque. She understands the nature of our predicament and spoke to her partners, and they have offered to buy us out. They will need your help for a couple of hours per week, simply with clerical things. That should be enough to satisfy your internship."

My eyes swelled, not just at the reality of Uncle Jack falling on a sword I helped lay, but also at the collapse of the life Doug built here. As long as he was in the Midcoast, he'd be tied to Uncle Jack. I wasn't surprised that he felt like this was the only way out. My uncle must have agreed. I nodded and finally spoke up.

"Okay, I take it Shirley doesn't care about my role in this?"

"No," Doug said. "And because of that ridiculous stunt Jack pulled, and the acquisition of our remaining clients, everything Shirley knows will be covered under attorney-client privilege."

"Well, there's a rare win," I added.

Doug smiled. He explained that the acquisition would be complicated and that it could last well beyond my last few weeks. If something fell through, he offered to call someone on my behalf and vouch for a solution. Finally, Doug offered to tell me anything I wanted to know before he left, not knowing when or if we'd ever speak in person again under these circumstances.

"Yes," I replied, still with my desire for justice burning. "First, what's going on with Tracy Mitchell? Sam and I saw her the other day. She wanted you to help her talk to the cops?"

"Tracy's a tough cookie, Billy. But you know that I suppose. I'm not sure what to make of her, but I don't want her to become human collateral again. She'll be okay though I think."

I nodded, thought for a few seconds, and then moved on to my more pertinent question.

"Um, what would make Uncle Jack do all this?" I asked Doug. "I can't figure it out."

Doug paused, and looked briefly out the door, careful not to invite stray looks from the FBI agents.

"Your uncle loved having influence, but he was also scared of losing it for nothing. These people must have promised him something - maybe money, maybe more power."

I shrugged. Doug was right, but that didn't make sense if Jack was just going to give up his firm when he was caught. Whoever had a grip on him must have earned Jack's respect long ago.

"Huh," I said. "Uncle Jack has such a big ego, I guess I just never saw him selling out to anyone."

"Well Billy," Doug shook his head. "In the last couple of days, there's only been one person who I can think of that your uncle truly respected and feared."

"Who is that?" I chuckled slightly. I couldn't think of anyone, but Doug looked me straight in the eye.

"Trevor McGary," he said. "The Senator."

***

After Doug left and we did the obligatory handshakes and manly hugs, I sat outside on the stone wall and waited for Sam to arrive. However, my mind couldn't stop thinking about Doug's last conversation with me. The mysterious Senator McGary, who, despite his enigmatic Don Draper-like persona, was still one of the most popular politicians in the history of the state in only a few years. What the heck would he have to do with this? I knew Doug was politically minded and no fan of folks like McGary, but he knew better than to throw unleveled accusations with the feds in earshot. Perhaps he was just coping with the betrayal of his closest confidant, or maybe he was onto something.

After all, Jack and McGary had been classmates at Yale Law. They bonded over their Maine roots and desire for future success. But, as the story goes, somewhere along the way McGary found his gear in state affairs as a prominent businessman and general counsel, while Uncle Jack returned to the Midcoast, content being a big fish in a smaller pond. Through the years since they respected each other and stayed friends. And as far as I knew, McGary was the only friend of my uncle's more successful than him. Therefore, I couldn't see how anyone would be surprised if a string of favors went too far.

The one wrinkle in this hypothesis, should it be true, was the role of my friend and rival Adam Olsen. On one hand, it was extremely naive to think that a low-level intern would have a role in a grande cabal of conspiracy. But on the other hand, whipping boys like Adam are the first to be used as scapegoats or collateral damage. This was all becoming too complicated for me. Part of me would be thankful when I received my walking papers from Sam before I got caught in the crosshairs. Another part wished there was a better outcome.

I shook my head and skipped a rock down the sidewalk. Suddenly, Sam appeared around the corner and grabbed me by the arm.

"Come inside, Billy," he blurted.

We shuffled into the same side room as before, and Sam flashed his badge for the FBI guys who were still cleaning up. They had found nothing more here but were searching Jack and Nora's house simultaneously. Sam sat down in one of the remaining wooden chairs.

"More bad news, kid. The State guys found a hit on a car," Sam pushed a stack of papers toward me with grainy pictures on them.

"Okay? And? I thought you guys were done with me now," I sighed, completely over all of this despite my newfound concern over Sen. McGary and Adam.

"Well, do you see what that is?"

"I have no freaking clue, Sam. I really don't."

"It's a blue Ford Bronco, 2023. Parked at the Percival estate on May 25th," Sam pointed to the time stamp, then brought out his iPad to show me a video. "The State Major Crimes Unit got this security footage from your uncle's laptop at home. Shared it with our guys. Somebody sent it to him, we're thinking it was the Percivals themselves via Doug Courtier."

I stared at the pictures and the video, speechless. It made sense. Doug knew Tracy was too close to the situation but he also wanted to protect everyone, so he obtained and sent this video to Jack as a warning. Doug saw things were closing in on Jack. Rather than listening, Jack got spooked and doubled down despite what was revealed. However, these weren't any old images. They had much worse implications for me.

Sam saw me begin to squint further, so he paused the video clip.

"Billy," Sam said quietly. "This vehicle is registered to Dr. Peter LaMarre."

I nodded. "I recognize the car," I said, my voice shaking.

Sam resumed the video. A few more seconds passed with the car parked. Then a bigger man appeared near the passenger door, wearing a mask, and he violently shoved two adults into the back seat, who were previously hidden from the frame. Sam stopped and zoomed in with his fingers.

"You know who they are too, right?"

I nodded again, "Tracy Jackson and Jordan Mitchell."

Sam looked at me again. "Our girl Tracy wasn't honest with us the other day," he said.

"No, I guess not."

"The police will be at your friend's house within the hour to speak with Dr. LaMarre," Sam continued. "Someone was driving that vehicle. It could very well be LaMarre. I suggest you make a beeline home when you leave here. We'll catch up on the other side."

An FBI agent walked by and glanced at us chatting there.

I looked down at my backpack on the ground, Adam's YETI still nestled into the side pocket. If the LaMarres or Adam were truly in on this conspiracy, there'd only be one place they'd rendezvous. Perhaps I could kill two birds with one stone.

Fifteen

Camden traffic at the intersection of Route 1 and Route 52 wasn't nearly as bad as I anticipated. Within no time, I was en route toward Bayside, with my time at Bakeman & Courtier over quicker than a Bruins playoff run. The sun was hidden to my left, but still bright enough to cast beautiful colors onto the bay to my right. Motorists whizzed by in all directions, priming their plans for the weekend ahead. Each SUV that passed reminded me of Megan's Bronco, and ultimately the chaos that loomed. As I approached Lincolnville Beach, I made a tight-pin turn toward the LaMarre's. If Sam was right, the cops would be there in no time. And if Doug was right, there was a chance Adam could be too, in hopes of doing McGary's bidding. But if no one was there, I prayed for what Megan would learn when she returned home from the Dairy Emporium.

Their home grew bigger as my Jeep descended the inclined driveway. I noticed the Bronco there, perhaps a sign that Megan was home. I also noticed Adam's Nissan, hoping maybe he was oblivious to everything. My Jeep faced the exit, in case I had to make a clean getaway. Upon getting out, I walked toward the Bronco.

"Still admiring my new car?" a familiar voice called from the porch.

I turned around. Megan stood on the steps, her hair still tied back as if it hadn't been changed since she got home from work.

"Yeah," I said. "Still admiring."

'Well, don't look too long, or else it might ghost you for a week."

I laughed, "Sorry about that, I should've called."

"Billy, this isn't 1970, a Snapchat would've done the trick."

She walked toward me and reached for my hand. I shivered a little bit, thinking about last week.

"I'm glad I got sent home from work early and didn't miss you. I wondered if it was too much," she said softly.

"It's okay Meg," I replied. "Really. I wanted to see you too, but I was also hoping to give this to Adam," I pointed toward the Nissan. "He left it at the club."

I pulled the YETI out of my bag.

"He did mention today that he was missing it, but we haven't had a chance to talk much since, well, you know... Adam just got here."

Part of me thought she was talking about our make-out session last week or possibly even Jack's arrest, but maybe it was something bigger. That prompted me to look back toward the Bronco. I was hard-pressed for a time before somebody showed up. I should probably get out of here.

"Maybe I should leave you to it then – "

"It's okay to admit you have feelings, Billy," Megan interrupted. "I can tell you feel something for me just like I can tell you desperately want to drive that Bronco."

I laughed nervously.

"I'd let you take me out in it, you know, even if my dad says no at first."

I froze, knowing the link between the security footage and Peter LaMarre. "What do you mean?" I asked.

"It's a long story, but basically Adam dinged it up the first week I got it and since my dad pays for the insurance, only I can drive it now."

For a second I caught a breath of relief.

"Wait, but I don't see anything wrong with it," I replied.

"Follow me," Megan said, bringing me to the passenger side that was usually concealed when she parked it facing forward.

Could this have something to do with the Percivals' video? I wondered. Megan showed me a spot underneath the side mirror. It was dented and had yellow scuffs.

"See, Adam did this. Didn't see one of those big yellow signs that tell people to slow down. He hit it. My dad was livid."

I chuckled, but something didn't fit.

"When was this?" I asked.

"Oh, like I said. The first week I owned it. Actually, it happened a couple of miles from your house. Still waiting on an insurance claim..."

Oh shit. I thought. This had to be the vehicle that hit the sign the night I was fishing. Plus, I now knew it was the same vehicle that showed up on the Percivals' tape. Both were on the same night, and Olsen was driving it. Adam Olsen, Trevor McGary's intern. Two's a coincidence, three's a pattern, and four is a smoking gun on fire with rockets.

I looked back at the dent, but Megan was annoyed with my ongoing curiosity.

"Yep, the dent is huge and it's gonna cost us."

My face grew dim and she noticed.

"What's wrong Billy?"

I paused. It was now or never. Despite her romantic advances and the entangled mess that was quickly becoming a love hexagon, Megan LaMarre was still a sweet, smart, caring girl who deserved none of what she was getting. Everyone was lying to her, and I finally wanted to be done doing that.

Clouds began to gather and the sun started to fade behind them. I reached for her hand and brought her behind the Bronco out of sight from the house. In minutes, I explained all I could. First about Myles Jackson and how I found him, where I found him. Then, about Sam Wells. Then, about my uncle being arrested and about Doug's theory regarding McGary. Finally, about the security footage. Much like Tracy Jackson days ago, I watched Megan's face turn from curious, to confused, to angry.

"I can't believe you would insinuate criminal behavior on any of us, Billy - especially my Dad or my boyfriend. I don't care about your DEA friend. You're not actually James Bond, you know."

"Megan, listen. That's not true at all," I pleaded. "The cops are coming any minute now to question your dad. But since he's not here yet, who's to say what happens next, or what's already unfolded? These people are dangerous, and they're getting spooked. My uncle is lucky to be in jail and not dead."

I pointed to the dent in the Bronco. "The wolf is at the door, Meg."

Her face hardened.

"I don't blame your family at all," I pleaded again.

"Fine," she stuttered. "Come with me, but no more secrets now."

Megan brought me into the house and then to the living room. I overheard running water, presumably where Adam was showering. Hopefully, he was still naked when the cops showed up, just for added measure.

"We don't have much time," I insisted.

"I know, I know. Look," Megan replied, handing me Adam's unlocked phone. "See what you can find."

My eyes widened.

"Let's go, Sherlock. Tick, tock," she chimed.

I began in his Settings, using a little-known part of the software system that tracked frequently visited locations. Most of them were in Brunswick, Camden, Rockland, Belfast, or Portland. But Bayside Village, presumably at his cousin's house, had not been visited since last November on Thanksgiving Day. Rather, the Percivals place on Shore Road was visited three times, enough to be a significant location. I screenshotted this page, with May 25th being one of the days visited.

Further, I scrolled his call log and discovered he had received daily calls from an Unknown Caller the entire week leading up to May 25th. Finally, I opened a game application called HockeyStarsPlus.

"What the hell are you doing?" Megan whispered.

"One second, we play this all the time."

Megan sighed.

In the app, I scrolled over to in-app messages, which I know he uses frequently when we play one another. On TV shows, it's always the mobile chat rooms that have secret encrypted messages. Cops sometimes use them to eliminate alibis and catch criminals.

Evidently, Adam had one new message, from a bizarre alpha-numeric username.

15:23 - PirateBenny121579: GET your ass out of there. TMac is closing it down and looking for scalps.

I looked over at Megan. We both shrugged, but I screenshotted it anyway. The locations were enough to bring Adam in, but I broke many due process rules in obtaining the evidence so it was going to be inadmissible. "TMac" could easily be McGary but there was no hard proof of that. Likewise, the calls were all from unknown numbers. It was going to be hard. Suddenly, we heard the water shut off.

"You gotta get out of here too, Billy," Megan whispered.

"Please send –" I started to say.

"I will get them to you and delete the screenshots. Just get out of here."

I hustled back and into the Jeep. Only nine minutes had passed since I drove into their driveway. As I continued north into Bayside, police cruisers headed south.

Sixteen

The afternoon had been so eventful that I realized I never even ate my lunch. In fact, the past two days I had barely eaten anything. Mom and Dad were expecting me for dinner, but I had no idea when it would be ready. So rather than get home and pace around for two hours, I made a pit stop to keep the wolves away.

Right on the outskirts of the village, close to Route 1 lay Bayside Market, maybe about a half-mile from the golf club and a couple miles from Wakefield's. They mostly had pizza and sandwiches, which was far and away enough to do the trick. After I walked in there, I realized I hadn't been inside all summer. Growing up, it was a staple for youthful adventure, especially since it was safe to bike there before I could drive. As I got older and eventually obtained my license, my local friend groups decided that hanging out "in town" in Belfast or Camden was more fun than biking around Bayside. Perhaps not coming here was just a natural outcome of growing up, but it also could reflect how busy I was this summer working for my now-criminally-charged uncle and my new best friend the fed. I didn't have time to guess.

I stood in line at the counter, waiting for a surfer dude in front of me to finish buying his Corona 12-pack while another lady in front of him was getting scratch tickets. But before I could reach the checkout, I noticed Steve Hamilton over at the beer fridge. He quickly turned, saw me, and approached.

Only three years out of high school and it was still hard not to call him Mr. Hamilton. Steve was a great man, a real salt-of-the-earth guy. He was easily one of my favorite teachers and in fact, a true friend of Myles Jackson as well. I hadn't seen him all summer, and certainly not since Myles was killed. Steve walked up and extended his hand. We exchanged pleasantries. His Red Sox cap had faded from navy blue to gray and there was cut grass stuck to his jeans. This man was always working on something. I figured today was no different.

While I bought my pizza slice, we chatted about the summer weather, my upcoming fall plans at Dartmouth, and the like. He joked with me once during high school that he went to Dartmouth too, UMass-Dartmouth to be exact. That was always a good laugh during my senior year after I had been accepted. After reminiscing about that joke and ringing up my pizza, I stepped aside from the counter so we could talk more.

"So what're the Sox 'gonna do at the deadline, Billy?" Steve asked. "Any ideas?"

I shook my head. "Hard telling, big series coming up with the Yankees though."

"Yeah, that's true. I'm not sure we have the pitching," he replied.

"Me either, when do *you* go back to school?" I asked.

"You should know, Billy," Steve smirked, poking fun that I wasn't paying attention to my mom's schedule. "They're going back the Tuesday after Labor Day. I guess they'd had enough of that early start bullshit this year."

We both chuckled. “Don’t tell your mother I said that,” Steve added with a smile.

“I won’t.”

“But she probably hasn’t told you that I’m all done teaching, huh?”

“I didn’t know that,” I replied, shaking my head.

“It’s okay, there’s been a lot going on.”

I nodded. At age sixty-three, Steve Hamilton had given almost forty years to Waldo County. Like a big brother to Myles Jackson, he had likely been through the wringer also this summer. I didn’t blame him for calling it quits after these past few years, following the pandemic. Chances are he’d end up somewhere in the Keys or on the Cape with his boat, finally free from the toils of teaching us kids the Pythagorean theorem, sailing southside from the tentacles of Penobscot Bay.

Steve outstretched his hand again and thanked me for taking the time to speak with him. According to Steve, not a lot of former students still frequented his stomping grounds. He headed for the checkout with his beer, and I left for home. Despite all the severe circumstances of this summer, the local character had remained intact. Driving home, I hoped that wouldn’t change.

***

When I returned home, Lori was getting ready to go in for the late shift. Her tenure as a waitress had gone better than I thought these past few weeks, but I wouldn't dare tell her that. I set my phone down on the coffee table and began taking off my shoes.

"Hey Billy," she said. "I'm sorry about all this. You won't believe how hard I've been trying to avoid social media with all this crap going on."

I chuckled mildly. "Yeah, try me."

She stared at me for a second and then continued getting her hair ready in the foyer mirror. "So did you ever figure out what was going on with Adam and Megan? Seems like you've still been hanging out with them a lot this month."

I hesitated, Lori's voice sounded suspicious. "Oh you know, the usual bickering. I think they're fine now."

"They'll be fine until AO finds out you kissed her."

"What the hell are you talking about?" I tried my best not to sound defensive.

"You didn't think I recognized that mood of yours when you got home last weekend? You're lucky I hadn't said anything until today," she laughed.

I blushed and shook my head.

"It's okay, Billy. I'm sure he'd give you the first swing," Lori continued.

"Alright, enough already...It was a one-time thing."

My phone vibrated on the coffee table. Megan's name appeared. Lori looked down at the table, and she saw what I saw.

"Mmmmm," Lori smirked. "A one-time thing."

"Okay, I'm leaving now. Enjoy work."

Lori mouthed something I couldn't translate before walking out the door. No matter what happened, I could count on Lori to tease me. I'm glad she had a job to go to, but I am even more relieved to know Milton will be keeping an eye on us all.

I went upstairs to my room and opened the text. To no surprise, Megan had followed her end of the bargain. Her tact was appreciated because the allotted time since I left her house allowed me to figure out my next move. The three images I needed were attached, though she also included two text bubbles below them.

Here you go. I will delete this text from my end after it's been delivered. Sorry, I didn't believe you. Good luck. The cops are talking to my dad.

Thx - sorry about all this

At dinner, my family tried talking about other things. I mentioned running into Mr. Hamilton at Bayside Market. Mom pondered if Lori would work again during the fall semester at Orono. My dad wasn't talkative at all and didn't care much for our conversation. I couldn't blame him knowing reality was setting in tonight. Before bed, I turned off the Sox. Colorado was winning by four runs following another bullpen implosion. That didn't bode well considering the Yankees were up next on the schedule. I went to the porch to turn the outside light off, mostly because the moths could be a nuisance this time of year.

As I stood there, I listened in the distance. I could faintly hear voices and vehicles from Shore Road or Route One. Crickets were what I heard mostly. The moon was high and bright, just as it had been two months ago at Kelly Cove. I wondered if Uncle Jack felt any guilt about what happened to Myles that night. Jack wasn't an evil person, so I bet he did. Nothing he would have gained from Kidd, McGary, or the cartel was worth someone's life. He may have done it to protect us or his firm. Maybe someday I will find out.

In the same breath, I suppose that's why Tracy lied to Sam and me about the cartel blackmailing them. Maybe that's why Jordan was so eager to fall on the sword. Kidd didn't care about their love affair, he just wanted to make sure nobody else talked. And to do so, he kidnapped them and blackmailed them that night at the Percivals. Someone was driving the car though. It could've been Peter LaMarre, but it was probably Adam Olsen, another scapegoat whipping boy caught in this spiderweb at the hands of powerful men.

I planned to bring what Megan sent me to Sam's hotel tomorrow, hopefully before anything else happened. By now, Conrad Kidd and possibly even Trevor McGary could be onto us. Time was of the essence, but Sam and I would need a plan - what I found was only circumstantial and not obtained properly. My gut said we would need to set another trap. The only question is if Sam would let me back in for one last kick at the can.

***

In the morning, I opened an email from Shirley Levesque. She didn't want me to start with her firm until next Monday, which meant for the next week I would be unemployed. My earnings this summer were modest, but the pay reduction certainly hurt, especially considering that I had expected to be working with Jack and Doug more than usual. That was the bad part.

The good news was that it gave me a rare Wednesday off, which was perfect for closing up the loose ends with Sam Wells. Before I could leave the house though, my mom lurked downstairs in the kitchen, as if she was waiting for me.

"Morning Billy," she said softly.

"Hi, Mom. Just us today?"

"Yeah, unless you have plans with Jason Bourne or whatever," she smiled nervously.

"Not yet," I chuckled.

"Lori is with Molly, and Dad is well, doing his thing. No days off."

I shook my head and opened the fridge to get some OJ. While I poured, we talked about school and what I had read from Shirley. I expressed that I was worried about what would happen if I didn't get my internship hours. All of this mattered to my future law school applications. To be honest, since Monday I hadn't given much thought as to how this all would impact my candidacy. Part of me wanted to bail for Pepperdine or Vanderbilt rather than stay in the Northeast where people could know Jack, let alone Trevor McGary. If I put Johnson, Ricker & Levesque on my applications instead of Bakeman & Courtier, maybe that would help.

"You know Billy," Mom added. "It's okay if you're not an attorney."

As usual, she was right. Nobody said I *had* to be a lawyer. Only I had ever wanted that dream. I pictured myself leaving Bayside one day and forging my own path elsewhere in Maine or the country. But there were also times when I pictured myself taking over for Jack and carrying on the legacy of Bakeman & Courtier here in the Midcoast. Now, I wondered what legacy there even was anymore.

News had yet to break publicly about Uncle Jack, but word had got around where it mattered. Jack was to be disbarred. No other arrests would be made until they figured out who was driving the

Bronco. Peter LaMarre was questioned, but all signs pointed to Adam as the driver as far as I was concerned. AO could be brought in at any moment. All the public knew was that Tracy Jackson was now a person of interest. What they didn't know is that she was largely innocent and that the real fault lay at the hands of Conrad Kidd, this unnamed motorist, and possibly Senator McGary - rather than Tracy and Jordan. Eventually, I believed it would all come to light and our family name would be associated with one of the darkest moments in Maine's history.

I brushed off Mom's concerns and told her that this experience only fortified my commitment to truth and justice. She reluctantly acquiesced and explained she was going to the sunroom to read. Once she was heavily into a Jane Austen novel for the eightieth time, I decided to go see Sam and finish the job.

***

My tires squealed into the parking lot at the Captain's Retreat, the same way they had weeks ago. Instinctually, I went to the bar, where Sam and I had first concocted our plan to nail Conrad Kidd. But after weeks of failing to find the evidence to get him, our best chance was to close the walls around him using what we had learned the past couple of days.

Sure enough, Sam sat in the exact same booth as before. Before I could even speak, he let out a big sigh.

"For God's sake, Billy. Do you want to tell me why you're here and not out of the country yet? These guys could be onto you any moment now."

We both knew that was an exaggeration and likely not true, even though time was ticking.

“Look, Sam,” I reached for my phone. “Adam is an accessory. I have proof.”

He examined my phone and the pictures I still had in my camera roll.

“Where the hell did you get this shit? Adam folded on you that fast?”

“Not exactly.”

Sam's eyes widened.

I continued, “I went to the LaMarre’s –”

“Freaking brutal, man.”

“Let me finish - I went to Megan’s last night. I told her about us. About everything.”

He glared at me. “Did you bring her a ring while you were at it?”

“Shut up,” I scoffed. “Her Bronco, *her dad’s Bronco,* has a big dent in it. She said Adam was driving it the night Jackson disappeared.”

“So you’ve been schlepping around with her all summer and just now, on July 25th, she’s gonna let out that detail?”

“I guess so, it’s unbelievable,” I sighed. “So anyway, I explained what was going on and she brought me Adam’s phone. He had encrypted messages on there,” I pointed to the next image.

“Alright, I see that,” Sam replied.

“I think Adam drove the Bronco at the behest of Conrad Kidd and ultimately Trevor McGary.”

Sam nodded slowly, taking it all in. "And you don't think your girl is just covering for her dad?"

"Did I ever try to convince you to think otherwise of my Uncle?" I challenged Sam."Loyalty in this town was gone the second Tracy Jackson planned a trip to Hyannisport with Jordan."

"Or the second you started sneaking around with that girl behind that other dufus's back."

"Don't you start too..." I scoffed again.

Sam chuckled but agreed. "Okay," he said. "We can talk to your buddy based on circumstance, but that's not enough. Not unless young Wayne Gretzky over there says he was driving the Bronco with intent to aid the murder. Pete LaMarre could've already revealed that, so we need to get to Atkinson first. Otherwise, it's just a coincidence that the Bronco is busted. The Percivals' footage Jack received doesn't show the driver or Kidd."

I gritted my teeth. Sam was right.

"And McGary," Wells continued, "That's another story. We can't just go walking around like Doug Courtier and accuse sitting United States senators of murder."

Sam was right again, as I expected. I didn't want to bring it up first, but I knew what he was going to suggest next.

"Then maybe we just gotta hope Adam talks about his boss," I said, luring Sam into what I knew his preferred method of getting information was.

"No Billy, let's just trap both these guys with their own kind of bullshit."

Seventeen

The night I first met Sam Wells, my family had gone to Neptune's on the Belfast Waterfront to celebrate my father's birthday. The restaurant was owned by a man named Owen Yates, one of my former baseball coaches, and his wife Melissa. One time, my buddy Hank from high school and I returned lost money to their restaurant and were forever heralded as heroes in their eyes. This time, though, I would need a favor from Owen if my plan with Sam Wells was to work.

From the get-go, our plan was going to be very risky but the concept was simple. I was to arrange with Owen Yates that a private room at Neptune's would be left vacant for a short time. In that short time, I would meet with Adam at the bar for a casual beer or two. Meanwhile, in exchange for partial exoneration, Uncle Jack would lure Senator McGary into the private room at the same point in time. Jack's cover would be that the invite was to expose who caught on to him, but in reality, Sam and his DEA agents would be undercover as nearby patrons. Then, I would enter with Adam and blow up the whole thing. Sam and I would then pretend we turned both Uncle Jack *and* Kidd, hopefully convincing McGary to confess. Adam would be left with no choice but to confess too. Finally, when we later revealed to McGary that Kidd wasn't cooperating with us, we believed McGary would crumble and give up Kidd's whereabouts.

We believed this plan would implicate the accessories involved with the murder of Myles Jackson, including the other passengers in the Bronco. At this point, there was no reason to think Peter LaMarre was aware of who was in his daughter's vehicle except possibly Adam, but we needed this plan to prove it. If we failed, then our lives and the lives of Jordan and Tracy could be in danger. McGary was a politician after all, so if he called our bluff and contacted Kidd after the fact, it was all over. Our cover was blown and so was everyone else.

Similarly, if McGary truly had no idea, then he could easily use his political power to make Sam Wells, Roger Atkinson, U.S. Attorney Patricia Marvin, and District Attorney Marcus Jefferson unemployed for life for making such accusations. In addition, my career as an attorney could be over before it even began. But no matter what happened, we risked turning this place, known for charm and beauty, into the site of the decade's most significant political scandal.

Sam received confirmation from Putnam and Marvin that the operation was to take place on Friday afternoon. Uncle Jack had posted bail and agreed to take part in the operation as part of the deal. Should we succeed in catching Kidd and McGary, Jack would be free from prison but never able to practice law again. That was a trade he was willing to make, according to the prosecutors. My assignment was to convince Adam we needed to hang out, which could be difficult if he suspected anything of me, whether related to McGary or Megan. The second assignment was to go talk to Owen Yates.

Thursday afternoon I strolled into Neptune's after parking slightly up the road between Gillie's and the local shoe store. Coach Yates was arranging bar glasses under the famous trident display.

They looked to be between lunch and dinner rushes. A few diners casually hovered nearby, telling fishing stories.

I approached Ben with a smile on my face. He turned.

"Billy, great to see you!" he exclaimed, tossing a kitchen towel over his shoulder and extending his hand.

"You too, Coach," I replied.

"Can I get you a drink, buddy? After what you did for us a few years ago it might as well be on the house."

"No thanks, but I could use your help with something else."

"What's going on?"

"Is there *any* way you could reserve that room for us tomorrow afternoon?" I pointed toward the small room off of the bar area, behind where a big lobster tank held their most precious inventory.

"You got a big crowd? We'd need you out of there by 5 for a rehearsal dinner. Some bride and her man from Connecticut or something."

"Uh," I stuttered, "We only got five people max anyway."

"I should be able to do that," Owen replied, thinking it over. He took off his Phillies cap and scratched his head. "How about 3 o'clock?"

"That sounds fine," I pulled out a crisp hundred-dollar bill as collateral. "This is me saying I won't let you down, Coach."

Owen shook his head and pushed my hand back. "I have no idea what you're up to Billy, but after giving us back what you found that day, Mel told me to never take anything from you again."

We both laughed.

"I'll see you tomorrow, Owen - uh, I mean, Coach."

"Sounds good brother. Just remember, I was the one who told you to focus on baseball and get off those ice skates."

"Yes, you did," I chuckled and headed for the door, thanking him one more time.

Phase one was complete.

***

Following the visit to Neptune's, I sent a quick text to Adam from the Jeep and invited him for beers on Friday afternoon. I thought he might need some coaxing, but within a minute, he answered.

Sure, let's do it. I gotta do it early though. Meg and I have plans tomorrow night.

Early was perfect, so I replied quite fast. I hoped Megan was being careful.

Sounds good. Meet at Neptune's at 3? Are you working?

Nobody in the government works on Fridays, why aren't you working again?

I thought for a minute, wondering if he was aware that Peter had been questioned by the cops yesterday. Atkinson might have convinced Peter to keep Adam in the dark about what was going on or vice versa. At this rate, everyone was trying to keep their cover. I began typing again on my phone.

Long story, let's catch up tomorrow

Adam sent a thumbs-up emoji and a beer glass emoji.

***

At twenty minutes to three on Friday, I walked back toward Neptune's. The Jeep was far up Main Street, closer to the Post Office. I was pretty tired, but the walk downhill toward the restaurant got my adrenaline going again. Sleeping the night before was not cutting it but my run earlier in the day had cleared my head.

Because we were in Belfast, Milton was briefed and Atkinson was involved in gathering the players so to speak, but this would primarily be run by the FBI and DEA at Putnam's direction. Both parties hoped to get Kidd for murder and drug trafficking. My parents knew about the operation and were assured locally by Atkinson and Milton that I would be okay. Only Sam, Uncle Jack, and I would be at the restaurant before 3 o'clock. A trio of undercover agents were to join Sam in the restaurant soon after, disguised as patrons. Their signal to me would be matching blue Under Armour sneakers, worn by all three agents. Putnam was to be in plain clothes on the boardwalk with two other agents on standby in a civilian car. Uncle Jack was supposed to show up before McGary. I would sit so that Adam could easily see McGary enter the private room.

I wore an earpiece and a wire disguised under my cap and my hair. Unless Adam got up in my face, he wouldn't see anything. When I approached the entrance, I saw Owen Yates again who waved. At first, he seemed confused that I wasn't going into the private room, but I explained that I was meeting a friend at the bar until the rest of our company came. Sure enough, Adam entered a few minutes later, sitting down with me so he was facing the door.

"Hey Adam, what's up?"

"Oh, nothing much Billy," his eye caught the mug display above our heads, a clear reminder of my favor. "Thanks for the Yeti by the way. Megan told me you dropped it off the other day. That was a great tee shot too."

"Oh thanks, I was just trying to match my dad."

"Looked like you were trying to prove a point for sure," Adam replied.

There was a twinge of bitterness in that comment. I decided to shake it off and act normal. After all, I didn't have the luxury of emotion today.

"How is Megan by the way? We didn't get a chance to talk much," I said, steering the conversation her way despite my best instincts.

"She's good. You wouldn't believe it though," Adam paused and looked around before lowering his voice. "Her dad got questioned by the cops."

"What for?"

"Some security tape. To be honest I don't know..." His voice trailed.

I couldn't tell if he was bluffing. Only Megan or her father could have revealed what was going on with the Bronco, and neither would have much to gain from that. Mr. LaMarre didn't even like Adam as far as I knew. The more likely situation was that Adam knew the events were connected to his little joy ride in May and he was spinning wheels, literally. The fact that he was on edge gave that away, however, he certainly couldn't have known what I was up to unless Megan spilled it. I trusted Megan too much to think that, despite how much I had kept from her myself.

"That's messed up," I replied.

Adam nodded and asked Owen for an Allagash. I ordered a Shipyard.

I heard the bell attached to the door behind me and looked over. It was nobody I recognized, but then I saw his blue Under Armour sneakers were a tell that he was one of the undercovers. We returned to sipping beer and chatting.

"So what are you and Megan doing tonight?" I asked.

"We're going to that lobster shack in Lincolnville. She's been asking me to go there with her all summer. Last time I was late, and well, you know how that turned out."

I winced. "Yeah, never be late."

In an instant, my comment reminded me that Uncle Jack and McGary should be here any minute themselves. I hadn't even looked for Sam yet either. I casually turned my head toward the back patio and then back toward Adam.

"*Don't worry, Billy, I got eyes on you,*" Sam's voice chirped in my ear. It startled me and I had to regather my thoughts quickly.

"You alright, dude?" Adam asked.

"Oh, yeah, fine."

Then the doorbell clattered again. It took every ounce not to turn around and look. Thankfully, Adam did all the work for me. His eyes widened.

"What the hell is he doing here?" Adam whispered.

I twirled around and saw Trevor McGary walk through the front door. His dark blonde hair was combed back, and his blue dress shirt had the top two buttons undone. He wore navy pants and brown dress shoes, so I wondered if someone would think he was the father of the bride for the upcoming rehearsal dinner and not a United States senator. Part of me thought he would follow the lead of Pennsylvania's senator and show up in a hoodie to blend in, but that wasn't the case.

Before I could look back at Adam, I saw a second guy walk in behind McGary, clearly a part of his entourage. The plan was already going haywire, as Uncle Jack hadn't arrived yet and this other man wasn't supposed to be here with McGary. I began to wonder if we were the ones being hoodwinked.

"I don't know what he's doing here," Adam scoffed, visibly shaken. He knew something was up.

"Yeah, me either," I replied. "Should we go say hi?"

Adam shook his head no and I looked back at the men standing in the foyer. A hostess led them into the private room. I only had a few minutes before Coach Yates realized I wasn't with the group yet and came back over to the bar. If Jack didn't show up soon, someone would have to intervene to keep these guys here. A U.S. Senator wasn't going to wait all afternoon.

"Who's the other dude?" I asked Adam, "You know him?"

"Uh, that's Ben Hornigold. He's the deputy chief of staff. He hates that he's not in D.C. full-time."

"Interesting," I replied, glancing back at Sam's perch before sipping my Shipyard. Something didn't add up.

"Alright Billy," my earpiece chimed in, with Sam's voice. *"I'm going to make a move on these guys. If Jack shows up, I'll just pretend I am with him."*

I made eye contact across to Sam on the deck and watched him get up from his table.

"Keep your buddy occupied until my signal. I ordered you guys some onion rings – incoming."

A server stopped by seconds later and handed off a plate of onion rings. Adam asked if I had ordered them, I lied and said it was before he got here. He began eating and I listened to Sam in my ear:

"Senator, good to meet you." Sam greeted McGary in the private room.

"Likewise, uh, are you with Mr. Bakeman?" McGary replied.

"Yes, we're very close."

"In what capacity?"

"Associate. I've been keeping tabs on the situation since his arrest, and well, let's say I have a good idea of who we're dealing with."

I almost threw up an onion ring, but I kept Adam's attention despite his obvious paranoia surrounding the people in the restaurant. However, I too was uneasy. At any moment, he could turn on me just as quickly. There was no predictability now and we were all bluffing.

"Is that so? You're not that snake Doug Courtier by chance?"

"No, sir. I can't believe what that man did to Jack," Sam observed but continued. *"But I believe we're dealing with something more serious."*

There was silence for a few seconds. I grimaced.

"Alright, well let's figure out how to end it before someone else has to get arrested," the Senator said flatly.

"Well, let's start with Conrad Kidd," Sam declared.

"I don't know who that is," McGary replied.

I worried he was playing Sam.

"No bullshit, here, Senator. But I've already met Kidd and he told us to come see you."

Sam was incredible. I kept chewing my food while Adam finished his beer.

"Listen, buddy," McGary interjected. *"I don't even know who you are and you are very close to crossing a line you don't want to cross. Tell me where the hell Jack Bakeman is, right now."*

Sam would later inform me that Hornigold revealed he was carrying a pistol, and that the threat was grounds for his eventual arrest too.

"I don't know where Jack is, but I can tell you who I am. My name is Sam Wells, I am a special agent with the DEA. We have Kidd in custody on major federal crimes including interstate drug trafficking, tax evasion, and money laundering. My friends at other agencies are investigating a murder in the first degree. We need your help to solve this case."

I could hear McGary's smug voice laugh off Sam's introduction.

"Ben, let's get the hell out of here before you shoot this asshole."

"You don't want to do that," Sam said. *"I've got eyes around here and you and your paper boy have already threatened a federal agent. Try again."*

"You have some goddamn nerve accusing me of any wrongdoing, Agent Wells. I have committed my future to public service. I don't get involved in these petty affairs. And I sure as hell don't deal with murder cases."

"Tell that to Myles Jackson," Sam challenged.

I would later find out that Hornigold had visibly looked down, a tell that Sam had hit a nerve.

"I have no idea who that guy is, I've never met such a person."

"Sort of like how you didn't know Conrad Kidd and then got hot and bothered when I told you I met him?"

"You're a sad excuse for an agent, Mr. Wells. Wait until I tell the Attorney General that he has a wannabe Barney Fife in his ranks at the DEA."

"Senator, you can make veiled threats all day long, it doesn't bother me. The only person you're hurting is yourself, and people like Adam Olsen who believe in you."

"You're a pathetic idealist," Hornigold laughed at Sam. *"Your badge is gonna be in the garbage by morning. Come on, Senator - let's get out of here. This guy is a con artist."*

"No Ben, let's see if he has the balls to go further. Tell me, Sam. What am I —"

"Hey Billy," Adam interrupted my audio feed. "I'm gonna go take a piss, I'll be right back."

I was quickly losing control of AO. From inside the private room, Sam saw us get up. I didn't hear what was said in between.

"Get him in here, Billy," Sam instructed, not afraid of exposing anything now that he had brought up Adam's name.

I followed behind Adam. As we passed the private room, he tried to look the opposite way to avoid McGary, but McGary made eye contact with us. Somehow, without hesitating, I walked in first. Adam had no choice but to follow me.

"Hello Senator," Adam greeted nervously.

"Take a seat, kids," Sam ordered.

"Who are these guys?" Hornigold asked.

"Cut the bullshit, Ben," McGary snapped. "Tell me, Agent, why is my intern here for your little charade?"

Adam didn't look confused. Perhaps he expected this would happen someday. I sat there next to him, amazed at how the five of us in this room had stayed composed long enough to not cause a scene here at Neptune's. I would need to find Coach Yates more lost money after all this was done.

"Funny you ask, Senator." Sam looked over to me as if to include me, "We were expecting you to notice those two when you got here. You didn't see the kids and you also let a few undercovers sneak by, which is fine."

"I am going to leave now and have you fired in ten seconds unless you show me why I shouldn't," McGary replied.

"You're free to go anytime, Senator. I'm just curious why you haven't yet. Maybe you're looking for a way out?" Sam asked. "A way out that Jack Bakeman was supposed to provide?"

"What could you possibly mean by that?" McGary scoffed.

"A way out of using your gopher here as a fall guy. A way out of using your office as a shield to conduct foreign drug smuggling. A way out of using your friends to do your dirty work. A way out of life in prison."

So much for not accusing Senators of crimes.

"You're ridiculous, Agent Wells. I'm leaving and you will be out of a job at best."

McGary and Hornigold went to leave, but Adam piped up.

"Sir, you can get that guy canned, whoever the hell he is, or you can fire me, I don't care. Just let's end this whole thing before someone else has to get hurt."

"You idiot," McGary muttered.

"Buddy," Sam interjected. "I'm a federal agent, and your friend Billy here is my consultant. We know what you did, but it sounds like you're the one who wants a way out."

I looked over my shoulder out the window, the two uniformed agents were on the front walkway. McGary was trapped. Hornigold reached for his gun. Sam, out of nowhere, reached for his firearm from under his sport coat. My pulse thickened. This had *not* gone according to plan. Thankfully, Coach Yates hadn't seen this unfold, and all the patrons were preoccupied.

"Everyone sit down!" McGary shouted, interrupting what could have been disastrous and tragic. I guess his better angels were beginning to prevail.

Who I thought was a waiter walked in and asked if everything was alright. I glanced down at his shoes. Blue Under Armour. He stayed put.

McGary walked toward me, then paced back toward Sam.

"I, I don't know what's going on," Adam croaked.

"Look, no one's gonna get hurt, kid," Sam replied.

"Okay, Wells. I'll play ball," McGary started again. "Conrad Kidd is a scumbag. I thought he was my friend. Had been for years.

But he tied me all up in a web of his. Drugs from the Maritimes. I thought it was on the up and up, but he used my status for his gain. I was fooled and I cut him off."

"That's not what he told us, Senator."

"Well, what did he tell you? Or did he even tell you anything? I'm not convinced that Hornigold wouldn't be able to call him right now."

I froze. We were somewhat screwed if that cover was blown. But, as usual, Sam Wells had a contingency.

"Well, if you do call him you can ask him about the payments we've been sending him since June. He's been working for us."

Sam pulled out his phone and showed a deposit history from the DEA into a personal account, presumably belonging to Conrad Kidd. To my knowledge, he wasn't a criminal informant but I wondered if he could've been Sam's first source all along. More than likely though, this was a wild card Sam intended to play if things went south. I looked over at Adam, who was stone-cold silent for once in his life.

McGary laughed nervously, still pacing the room. Hornigold desperately wanted to get out of there.

"Mr. Hornigold," Sam asked. "Do you have any interest in calling Mr. Kidd now?"

He shook his head no.

"Jordan Mitchell," McGary interrupted. "He's the one who killed Jackson. Everyone knows that. Even Jack Bakeman knew that. That imbecile."

Everyone gave the Senator a blank look, so he continued.

"Tell me, gentlemen, did Jack Bakeman really put you guys on us so he could get back at me for being more successful? What a joke. You guys don't have shit. A few circumstantial names and a couple of supposed bank deposits. You guys won't give up the chance to put Kidd in jail, and Jordan Mitchell is already behind bars."

"Jordan didn't kill him," I interrupted. They all looked back in my direction. "And my uncle was smarter than you because he knew when to get out."

"Bakeman..." the Senator mumbled.

"You framed Jordan Mitchell to cover your ass," I continued, staring right at McGary. "And then you let Jack hang to dry because you believed he would never turn on you."

Sam went to interrupt me but I held my hand up.

"It's true though," I added. "My uncle didn't turn on you, but that doesn't matter. Kidd told us he blackmailed Tracy and Jordan at your direction."

All along, I had suspected that Tracy was the key. She never fully sought justice for Myles and still hasn't publicly revealed the affair. She also lied to us about their whereabouts, concerned that the discovery of such details would threaten their lives. A silence that was bought and paid for by Trevor McGary. Saying so was a risk to our desired outcome, but at this point, I was feeling so much adrenaline again.

"That's ludicrous, son. Did your uncle teach you how to tell stories like that?"

"No, Senator. My dad taught me everything I know."

"Ah, Marty's boy. Always the little man," McGary scoffed. "Listen, there's absolutely no proof to what Conrad is telling you assholes. Neither of us has ever met that couple."

"Did Billy even say they were a couple?" Sam retorted.

McGary looked uneasy, he had cornered himself. I shot a glimpse at Adam and made eye contact. Back when we played youth hockey together, Adam always had a way of reading the play before it unfolded. He found his way to where the puck was going, not where it was. I hoped he would do the same here. Thankfully, he came through for us. He must've been scared to death.

"I've met them," Adam spoke up. "They were in the Bronco that you guys had me steal."

Sam and I exchanged looks. Sam urged him on while Hornigold and McGary groaned.

"I was told to drive Kidd to Bayside. He would take care of the couple, but he wanted to intimidate them first."

"How so?" Sam asked.

"Kidd wanted to have Mitchell and the wife see Jackson get killed, wanted the last thing Myles saw to be his wife scared to death with the other man. But then we saw another car and we had to improvise. We didn't want to get caught. I sped off."

"Then what?" Sam continued.

"Connie Kidd stole a truck and went to kill Myles. When it was done he took the body back to Kelly Cove, but I couldn't believe it was done so fast. Then I circled back and we grabbed those two at the Percival mansion. Brought them back to Jackson's house."

"Who is 'we'?" Sam pressed. "I count that Conrad Kidd is long gone by now."

“Him,” Adam replied, pointing at Ben Hornigold. “I just drove while he told the wife and Jordan that they’d be dead unless Jordan admitted to killing Mr. Jackson.”

Hornigold sat still. I expected him to reach for his pistol, but that would’ve been a suicide mission for everyone, including his boss the Senator. Perhaps Hornigold realized that too.

“Interesting,” Sam asked. “Have to admit, that got by me.”

“Adam, who introduced you to Conrad Kidd?” I asked.

“Ben did.”

“Not Senator McGary?” Sam pressed again.

“Not at first.”

“So Mitchell was the fall guy for Kidd, who was the fall guy for Hornigold, who was the fall guy for McGary?”

Adam nodded.

“So what does that make you?” Sam asked.

“A dead man if he ever talked like this,” McGary cut him off, shaking his head. “Collateral damage. That’s what I surrounded myself with. I have plausible deniability for it all. Proof is what you don’t have for me.”

“Your reputation won’t survive either trial, not once we have testimony from everyone. Your fingerprints are everywhere.”

“Good luck with that, Agent Wells.”

McGary finally got up to leave.

“One more question,” I said. The Senator turned back. “What does Kidd have on you? He wouldn’t admit it, but I figured if you did we could arrange something for him.”

In my life, from Bayside to Hanover, I learned that *everything* was negotiation. From choosing a restaurant to truth or dare, it was always a multi-level calculus. And for someone like McGary or even Uncle Jack, it was also an analytical decision. Someone as powerful as McGary would only be worried about losing power, just as Doug had said about Jack and the firm. A big fish like McGary would do anything to stay in the pool.

"You're lost, kid. That guy is a scumbag and I hope he rots."

"Well, it's funny you say that Senator," Sam replied. "We don't have him yet, but I'm sure after this whole rendezvous we could certainly follow you right to him."

"You wouldn't dare," McGary scoffed.

"Then go ahead and leave," Sam said. "If you don't think there's a risk. I'm certain Kidd would open right up if given the chance at immunity."

"You're bluffing Wells," Hornigold interrupted.

"Try me."

Hornigold set his hand on his sidearm.

"Enough, Benny, you would miss them from this distance." McGary walked back into the center of the room and sat down. "I'll give it to you."

Eighteen

“Can I take a piss before this goes on?” Adam interrupted.

“Absolutely not,” Sam and Hornigold said in unison.

My pulse had quickened again, and I watched Senator McGary drift back to the table. He leaned down and set his hands on the table, but remained standing in balance.

“Alright,” McGary began. “Everyone listen carefully.”

Sam reluctantly nodded. Adam was probably going to wet his pants.

“This is how it’s gonna go,” McGary continued. “I am going to lead your agents to Kidd, and you are going to forget you ever saw me. You guys can get your man, ask him what you want, and Wells gets to walk away with a ribbon on his shirt – and I will disappear from this investigation.”

“Pat Marvin won’t go for that,” Sam interrupted. “The U.S. Attorney's office and the DOJ, we have too much at stake. We’ve now openly accused you, a Senator, of conspiracy. If we walk from you and that gets leaked, our reputation is ruined and the A.G. will have okayed a cover-up.”

“So naive, Wells,” McGary rebuked. “Don’t forget who you’re dealing with here. I can make it all go away.”

“No, you can’t. What, are you, uh, ‘ you gonna kill Conrad first?” Sam asked, chuckling.

McGary cocked his head. “That guy can go to hell, I don’t care what you do with him now.”

"Bullshit," I interrupted, immediately regretting it but continuing anyway. "Kidd could tell us something."

It had been two minutes of tiddlywinks and I hadn't received an answer to my question.

"No," McGary concluded. "He won't say shit. You think he's gonna trust the feds?"

I peered over at Hornigold, who hadn't said a word since McGary had verbally cucked him. Sam saw my eyes move.

"What about the paperboy?" Sam pointed over at Hornigold.

"He'd have Kidd, Mitchell, and the wife in a morgue by tomorrow if he was ordered to," I added.

McGary walked toward me and set his hand on my shoulder.

"Oh Bakeman," he said. "Loyalty and friendship is a beautiful thing, isn't it? I used to think that about your uncle. Would hate to see him get hurt too."

"More veiled threats –" Sam said, "in the presence of law enforcement..."

Hornigold cut them both off, "You know, boss. The funny thing about loyalty is that it's only as good as the best offer being made."

The Senator changed direction and cast his look on Ben Hornigold.

"You might be right, kid," Hornigold continued, looking at me. "Jack didn't turn on us. He's also not here like he was supposed to be. Jordan and Tracy didn't say a peep either, or else the feds wouldn't have taken this long to get here."

"Your point?" McGary interrupted.

"My point is, you had them all over a barrel," Hornigold looked over at Adam too. "They all sacrificed out of fear. But Connie Kidd doesn't fear anyone. Not even you. Are you gonna take the risk that the feds offer a better deal than us?"

"Better than his life? He's a dead man walking, bars or the stars." the Senator chimed.

"Well, so was Myles Jackson, but here we are still cleaning up that mess," Ben added. "Who knows what else Jackson did before Kidd killed him? So even if Connie's off the board, we're never gonna be clean."

McGary peered back toward Hornigold. "So what are you saying we do?"

"I'm not saying *we* do anything. If you're willing to betray Kidd now, what're you going to do to me, or Jack Bakeman? My loyalty is in the best deal."

"You idiot," the Senator chimed. "You'd never see outside a cell again if you go ahead with these clowns."

"You could have all the money in the world, Senator. All the power, and all the fame, but you won't be able to outrun it forever."

"Outrun what?" Sam asked.

"The cartels own *him*," Hornigold replied. "Not the other way around."

Finally, somebody was getting to the point, I thought.

McGary went to move on Hornigold but realized his deputy was the one armed. The Senator sat back down, clearly frustrated that his friend was now cucking him back. His house of cards was collapsing.

"Through their cronies, the black-market Canucks found out McGary was running an insider trading ring," Hornigold continued. "The Senator was investing in companies selling pharmaceuticals made in Canada. Then we were getting legislation passed that allowed for American imports and made those companies richer. Everything seemed clean until a cartel in New Brunswick found out. If an internal supply deficit was possible, they wanted a cut of the exports."

Lori had mentioned this legislation weeks ago.

"So then the syndicate up there had us by the balls," Ben sighed. "They threatened us, said they were gonna expose the trading ring unless they got a share, so that's when we reached out to my pal Conrad Kidd. We offered the Canadian cartel a new market of their own in exchange for cooperation. I had to stay out of D.C. to take heat off the Senator."

"You bastard," McGary scoffed.

I couldn't believe he was turning before our own eyes.

"But we needed help," Hornigold kept on. "We needed his old friend Jack Bakeman to run interference. He was gonna help us with the Coasties, the sheriffs, border patrol, and such. We wanted to infiltrate them all. Running contraband by night to Canada. Everyone would get richer.."

"But, then you ran into a problem," I added.

"Yes," Hornigold continued. "Kidd and the Canadians wanted better boats and we needed a skilled but under-the-radar builder. So we asked Myles Jackson, a well-connected man around here. We thought he was going to come through for us. He had all the makings of a great surrogate. The problem is Jackson was a veteran and didn't want to cross his old friends who were now in the Coast Guard, the CBP, or serving as cops."

"That was a miscalculation?" Sam asked.

"Yes," McGary hissed. "Jackson was a Boy Scout."

"But," Hornigold said. "We did some digging and realized his wife wasn't selling cookies door to door."

"She was sleeping with the Percival handyman, Jordan Mitchell," Adam interrupted. By now his bladder must've been in shambles.

"So you leveraged that?" I asked, secretly joyful that I had been right all along.

"They were both gonna be in the morgue if they talked," Adam said, "Just like me."

"You know," Sam added. "I dated a girl at the IRS when I was younger. She'd love to learn about all this unclaimed money, Senator."

"If you do that, this will all end badly for everyone. I promise that's not a threat, it's reality," McGary motioned to himself and Hornigold. "We'll go to jail, and all you clowns will be in the crosshairs of every corrupt crime boss from Springfield to Halifax."

"So what do you suggest we do?" Sam replied sarcastically. "Instead of taking your asses to federal prison."

"I'll plead guilty," Hornigold piped up. "As we said, the feds can have Kidd and he and I will go to prison. In exchange, I want an early release for cooperation."

Hornigold took a deep breath before continuing, looking over at McGary. "I will say Trevor knew nothing."

Sam and the other agent exchanged looks too. Certainly, the authorities and prosecutors may agree with such a proposal, and it would save face. However, even so, it would severely implicate McGary's reputation and risk the eventual revelation of his greater role in the whole conspiracy.

"Okay," Sam said. "Hornigold can help us get Kidd and with that, we'll close the whole drug ring, I suppose. The Mounties will appreciate the assistance there."

Hornigold nodded.

"But," Sam sighed. "I'm not sure how this ends for you yet, Senator."

"If you want to drain government resources and look into every cent I have, go for it. I'm willing to take my chances on that trial, and with Hornigold," McGary sneered. "He can fall on the sword, and like I said, I will always have plausible deniability and an alibi."

McGary was right, in many respects. The burden of proof was enormous and he had been in D.C. fighting for that legislation at the time of the murder. It could appear to some as an impropriety but it would be hard to prove. Others would look the other way and see a plain coincidence.

"Okay," Sam said, defeated in some respects. "I'll talk it over with Putnam and the Attorney's Office."

"What about these guys?" the other agent said, pointing to me and Adam. "Putnam is gonna want Billy to shut down finally, and well, the intern will serve time for willingly driving that getaway car."

Adam looked over at me. It was a look I had never seen from him. Doubt. Usually, AO was so confident and forward-thinking, but now he appeared defeated like Sam, though this time it was his own doing. Megan, Chamberlain, everything he had would be in jeopardy if his role was uncovered. And again, his bladder was still hanging on by a thread.

"Olsen won't serve time," Hornigold interrupted again. "I'll say I kidnapped him and made him drive."

McGary nodded. "Alright. This won't reach me then."

Adam let out a big sigh. Hopefully no urine came with it.

The rest of the room stayed quiet.

Sam outstretched his hand to Hornigold, who, only twenty minutes after threatening to shoot Sam, obliged and returned the favor. Adam thanked Hornigold several times. The other agent left the room with them both, and Adam probably went straight to the men's bathroom. The Senator didn't apologize to Adam or say goodbye to anyone. Instead, McGary left the room without saying a word.

I stayed behind with Sam, who told me this would probably be it for him in the Midcoast. No more late-night stakeouts in Belfast. No more sting operations in Camden. No more surprise visits to Bayside. From here on, Pat Marvin, Marcus Jefferson, and the authorities would handle the case's conclusion. His work as an investigator was over as far as Putnam was to be concerned. A special operations team would likely follow Hornigold and take in Kidd for questioning. Sam would finally check out of the Captain's Retreat Inn in the morning, and return to Boston shortly thereafter. I asked him if he would keep in touch with me.

"Only if I need a badass attorney who's a 40-year-old bachelor living with a dog," Sam replied, smiling.

I laughed too and shook his hand. So much of my time had been spent with Sam this summer that it felt like my internship had been with the DEA and not Uncle Jack's firm. In many ways, that was correct.

"Thanks for everything Sam," I replied a few seconds later.

"Anytime, Billy Bob," Sam patted me on the back and started to leave. "Good luck with your girlfriend!" he shouted as he was exiting the room, humming along to his newly-adopted Joe Diffie parody.

Suddenly, Adam appeared through the door.

"You have a girlfriend?" he asked.

"No, he's just being...I don't know."

"Oh well," Adam replied. "Seems like you guys got close."

I paused, assuming and hoping we were still talking about Sam Wells.

"Yeah, we did," I replied. "But so have you and I."

"True. I'm sorry about all this, Billy. I really shouldn't have lied to you. I messed up with these guys. I was so scared of them. All I ever wanted was to be important."

"I understand," I said, nodding my head. Adam didn't deserve this. He was a good dude, he just became caught up in feeling like he needed the approval of McGary or the LaMarres.

"So, what gave it away that I was the culprit? What made you lure me here?" Adam asked, his voice still shaking a little bit.

"To be honest dude, a lot of things."

Adam chuckled, "Wait, were you the guy in the Jeep at Kelly Cove?"

I nodded.

"Shit, man," Adam said, still stuttering. "Horrible timing. I don't know if I should be mad at you or not. Should have seen it coming, working for Jack Bakeman and all."

I nodded, still slightly feeling bad that I had kissed his girlfriend, hacked his phone, and lured him into an interrogation.

"You know AO," I started. "There's something I need to come clean about too..."

"Save it, Billy," he interrupted. "You got me fair and square. It's my fault. Just tell me one thing. Did you really want to be friends again, or did you know way back then that I was compromised?"

"Yes, I wanted to be friends. We ran into each other at the BMV and you guys invited me to that party," I laughed. "I had no freaking clue then."

"It's funny you say that," AO replied, looking out the window at the bay. "I knew even then that I was over my head. But I didn't know what to do. You were always so straight and narrow. As soon as I saw you that day, I thought you would know what to do."

"Really?" I asked.

"Yes, but then you said that you were working for the firm, and I remembered that Jack Bakeman was your uncle."

"So you thought I would learn what was going on?"

"I thought maybe you would end up on my side. But as time went on, you seemed oblivious to what I was dealing with. You stayed my friend..." Adam trailed off.

I chuckled, "Keep your friends close and your enemies closer."

Adam smiled and shook his head. He got up from the table and headed for the exit. We shook hands and said goodbye, mutually understanding that our friendship would forever be complicated. But before we made it through the main door, Adam Olsen had to get the last word one more time.

"Hey, Bakeman," he called.

"Yeah?"

"It's probably gonna be over with Meg and me soon," he said, nodding slowly.

"Oh," I replied, sounding as shocked as I could pretend to be after today's events.

"Yeah, it's okay, I guess. But remember Billy: just don't be late," Adam said back, tossing me a wink.

Then Adam Olsen disappeared behind the parked cars, reappearing to cross the street, where he later blended into a crowd of tourists.

From behind me, a familiar voice called out.

"You ever gonna tell me what the hell that all was in there?" Coach Yates clamored, cocking his eyebrow.

"No, sir," I replied, pulling out the one-hundred-dollar bill still in my wallet and passing it to him.

Owen Yates laughed, reluctantly taking the bill, and then he returned to the bar. "Buying the next round!" he exclaimed to the patrons.

I declined politely and made my way back through the front door. Then it was my turn to disappear into the crowd of tourists, where I would soon learn how difficult it was to blend in.

Nineteen

The last several days were some of the hardest of my life. For most of my adolescence, I believed in this place, my home. It was where I was completely safe to do whatever I desired, not a map dot surrounded by greed, corruption, and conspiracy. But yet that was the reality of human nature. In some respects, it was not unlike any other place. People were often driven by the same vices as in others. Jack and Adam wanted to be liked, Hornigold wanted to be trusted, and McGary wanted to be powerful.

That night, Mom and Dad didn't have much to say or ask me about. It was an unspoken understanding that I was mentally and emotionally drained. My father was also still reeling from all the uncertainty in his family. There was some talk that Jack would go to trial, though no one knew yet. A lot of it depended on what he provided the feds but he didn't show today. To cope, my dad poured into his work both at the office and at home for distraction, cooking a huge meal for us that night. However, my parents let me eat dinner in my bedroom and watch the Sox while they hashed over what to do next in the family. Helen and Marty were supportive of my efforts to bring justice, whether reluctant or not. Moreover, they were probably relieved that my part was finally over.

After the baseball game ended, I tossed and turned for what seemed like forever, thinking about the events that had unfolded. But when I heard Lori come home from work, I realized it was only half past ten. The television was still illuminating my bedroom, even though the sound was off. I got up and went to say hi to Lori, who still smelled like fried seafood.

"Hey Lori," I said, yawning. "Counting the days 'til Orono yet?"

"Hell yeah," she said. "If I have to serve one more lobster roll this summer I'm gonna lose it."

We both laughed.

"Hey," she continued. "My coworker told me there was some commotion up at Neptune's today. You know anything about that?"

I nodded and began telling the story. It was about time she knew the full truth, not just bits and pieces. Before I could even get all the players identified, a police cruiser tore into the driveway. Lori and I both went to peer out the window and quickly recognized Chief Milton emerging from the vehicle.

He stepped up onto the front porch, but I opened the door first anyway. Major Tom greeted me with a firm handshake and smiled at Lori. However, he soon grew a concerned look on his face.

"Hey, uh, kids," he said quietly. "Your folks asleep?"

"I don't know," Lori said. "Is everything okay Chief?"

"I'm afraid not," the chief replied.

Soon, Marty and Helen had heard the commotion and waddled over to the doorway. They joined us with grim looks as Tom began informing us of what had occurred.

Following the events of this afternoon, a joint task force descended on the property which Hornigold had given as a location for Conrad Kidd. While Tom couldn't tell us exactly where it was likely somewhere further east in Hancock County. When the authorities arrived, they found Kidd stone-cold dead. As a result, they looked for evidence of foul play in his home, only to find hundreds of thousands of dollars' worth of fentanyl, dozens of illegally obtained guns, several crates of ammunition, and copious amounts of nautical maps. Tom also explained that the agents found cash in both Canadian and American dollars, and account numbers of numerous offshore bank accounts. However, despite the trail of illicit activities, the authorities couldn't identify yet whether or not Kidd had been killed or if he committed suicide.

We stood there in shock, but Tom soon grew another concerned face, informing us of the fragility involved in this all and the serious need for discretion. Supposedly at the same time, a few state police officers had gone to do a check on Uncle Jack after Atkinson and other authorities were informed that he didn't show up at Neptune's. When the cops arrived at Jack's home, Aunt Bonny was gone too. As a condition of his bail, Jack was unable to leave Maine without permission. It got a little messy because the Jackson murder investigation was a state crime, but Jack's particular arrest had more to do with his role in helping Kidd, a case being handled primarily by the feds.

Tom believed that Jack and Bonny had fled home the night before, probably right under everyone's nose. Jack knew a lot about navigation and could probably evade law enforcement by sea or ground in the same way he had helped Kidd do so until Hornigold turned. My father was visibly worried for Jack's safety, but Tom assured Marty that he didn't believe anything bad would happen now that Kidd's world had crumbled.

Eventually, Chief Milton wrapped up the conversation and told us he was confident that the powers-at-be would have this concluded shortly. The others didn't seem so sure, but I trusted the chief's motives, even if a reunion wasn't imminent. Whether or not Jack was halfway to Bridgetown or Bathurst, I frankly didn't want to know. Fate and justice had already served him. There wasn't much more you could take from Jack Bakeman beyond his dignity and his reputation. In fact, there was only one man left standing who still had something to lose.

***

And so it went, a couple of days later I awoke to Lori and Mom watching the news again. This time Ben Hornigold stood on the steps of the federal courthouse in Portland, flanked by a handful of officers and the Assistant U.S. Attorney Patricia Marvin. Through the lenses of several live television cameras, and into the homes of thousands of Americans and Mainers, Hornigold publicly confessed to tax evasion, insider trading, conspiracy to commit murder, kidnapping, and reckless use of a firearm.

I sat there, sipping my orange juice, as Hornigold went on to list his grievances in a way that only Thomas Jefferson could do better. A few officers began to pull him away from the media scrum, but Hornigold piped one more time into the microphone.

"I am doing this for Jordan Mitchell, and Myles Jackson. And if you think the Senator is clean, look again."

From there, I looked over at my Mom and sister, our mouths agape. Ben Hornigold, in some sort of martyr-like sequence, had just publicly implied that Trevor McGary was complicit in high crimes too. Furthermore, Hornigold had unequivocally linked the death of

Myles Jackson to his verbal confession – a move that would surely link us all together forever. Someday, I wondered if Hornigold would be pardoned or freed for offering up McGary, but from that moment forward, everything changed. There was no longer a burden of knowledge to carry. As the weeks passed, we learned more about the fallout.

Canadian authorities used the information from Kidd's lair to help Maya Putnam and the DEA take down the rest of the syndicate in Saint John. Many were foreign nationals who never even held legitimate passports from the U.S. or Canada in the first place. So while Kidd had evaded folks here in the States for months to much dismay, he was not alone. Though his most insidious crime, the murder of Myles Jackson and the soon-to-be-exposed cover-up, is what drew the most ire from us in Bayside.

Jordan Mitchell was freed from jail, and all murder charges were dropped. The Maine State Police Chief, flanked by Detective Roger Atkinson and the Commissioner of Public Safety, held a press conference where they explained that Jordan Mitchell had been blackmailed and framed by the now-dead drug henchman Conrad Kidd and his government crony Ben Hornigold. Rumor spread that a *20/20* tell-all from Jordan's perspective would be filmed in the fall. The authorities also announced that Kidd died from an apparent self-inflicted gunshot wound. Some didn't believe it, and I remain skeptical.

However, conspiracy theories hit record levels when later that week, Senator Trevor McGary announced that he would be stepping down from his seat, citing the "distractions to the peoples' work."

Most inside and outside the Beltway knew that was code for the growing chatter about his role in Hornigold's confessed crimes and the possibility of a cover-up. Only Nixon could have done that dance better. In a few short months, McGary had gone from the most popular politician in the state to an infamous and corrupt scoundrel. Cable News couldn't get enough of that story.

Sara Lopez, Tom Milton, and the rest of the local law enforcement apparatus were never compromised by the cartel, despite McGary's grand plans. In all reality, it was simply one greedy Senator and his two henchmen, one of which would be going to federal prison while the other stayed on the run. Through it all, I was thankful for Chief Milton's steadfast devotion to safety and local order.

From Major Tom, I also learned that Sam Wells had been promoted within the DEA, taking the spot of Maya Putnam. Given her big win and the subsequent notch in her belt of uprooting the Gulf of Maine drug syndicate, Putnam had decided to run for Congress in Massachusetts. Sam was content to still be doing work on the ground, just as his father had modeled for him.

A memorial for Myles Jackson was erected at Belfast Harbor, and a regatta in Bayside was to be planned each year as a fundraiser in his honor. Proceeds would benefit teaching kids in the Midcoast to sail. My mother was unanimously appointed chair.

Facing public scrutiny, Tracy Jackson planned to sell the Jackson house just up the road from our home. I suppose that living there would simply conjure too many memories for Tracy's liking and that side looks from those who knew what she did eventually became too much to bear. I wondered where she may be heading instead.

In a similar feeling, I often think about what happened to Uncle Jack and Aunt Bonny. According to Dad, they were wanted by the U.S. Marshals in Canada, St. Pierre and Miquelon, the Bahamas, Mexico, and many other countries in the hemisphere. By the end of the summer, there was still no sign of them dead or alive. We all held up hope that they would return someday, even if it was to a foreign embassy for extradition. My father believed he was still alive, and that kept him hopeful. I didn't want to talk about it.

Miss Browning was exonerated of all wrongdoing and no one in my family could ever quite pinpoint why she cooperated with Jack's underground work. I also wondered why she told Megan's mother at the salon about what she knew. My best guess is that it was simply gossip run wild, which didn't surprise me. Most of the time all we ever had to gossip about around here was another weed store opening or another seasonal restaurant closing. We believed Megan's mom and Miss B. were no different. Miss B went on to work at Johnson, Ricker, and Levesque for a short while after my brief stint helping there, but neither one of us could shake the stench of previously working for thc now-fugitive Jack Bakeman.

The LaMarres were also cleared of any foul play despite the use of their vehicle to transport criminals. There were rumors that Peter was making a move to buy the Percival Estate now that the Percivals wanted to get the hell out of Bayside. To be honest, I'd prefer that Peter LaMarre and his daughter get to live there.

Megan and I texted a few times over the weeks that passed, but the initial flame had sadly died out even amidst her inevitable breakup with Adam. I pondered if it was for the best. After all, in a matter of days, I was heading back to Hanover, content to start my final year of undergrad.

That said, it would still be hard. Outside Megan and my family, I found it difficult to find someone who truly understood the personal nature of what happened this summer. Since the fallout with McGary, Hornigold, Jack, and Kidd, every true-crime podcaster and murder mystery superfan had been sending me emails at my school address wanting me to come on and share my stories. The events grew legs of their own. Cable news hosts wanted my family to share insight on the possible whereabouts of Uncle Jack. Reporters always called for comments. Streaming services were already talking about docuseries in development. Even people around town wanted to discuss it with us Bakemans any chance they could.

Furthermore, sleepy Maine was put on the map again for all the wrong reasons. A once celebrated Senator now resigned in veiled disgrace and facing possible prosecution. A once admired local businessman and Iraq veteran, was killed and now sensationalized as part of this phenomenon. And, a once postcard-like village, is now ground zero for a fever dream of new media. A place known for charm and beauty is now unmasked and perceived as untamed.

It was *not* how I imagined the summer would go. I never imagined an inquisition of this magnitude would happen here. Some locals relished the attention, but others like me prayed for the day when it would vanish.

***

The Sunday before Labor Day, we left the church and planned to go straight home, preparing one final time for *both* Bakeman kids to load their car and head back to college the next day. For many Mainers, Labor Day marks the end of the summer. After the service, my folks spoke briefly with the pastor about our family, of course sharing mutual concerns over Jack and Bonny. Lori and another girl were making plans to meet up in Orono next week. Meanwhile, I made a beeline for the car, still weary of small talk. Across the street though, I spotted a blue Ford Bronco, spotted and shined. A familiar face looked out through the window, smiling slightly and tossing a casual wave. I wandered over and Megan LaMarre rolled down the window.

"I figured I'd find you here," she said. "Glad I caught you before you left town."

I smiled, "Me too," I admitted.

Megan motioned for me to get in the car. I sat in the passenger's seat, remembering that our roles were reversed several weeks ago at the pond when we kissed. Internally, I was warmed by the memories of a perceived simpler time.

"You know, Billy," Megan said. "It doesn't have to be weird between us. What happened with you and Adam and the cops and stuff is what it is. For what it's worth, me and my parents are glad you did what you did before I got too involved."

"Really?" I asked.

"Of course," she replied. "Who's to say what would've happened if you hadn't gone full James Bond on us."

I smiled back at her. "Thanks, Megan."

"And, I'm starting at Colby-Sawyer next week. Finally put in my deposit at the last minute. I'm gonna try and get into sports medicine. My dad said no more 'slouching off' so I decided to try something new. He's thrilled actually."

"That's awesome, my buddy Hank goes to Colby-Sawyer. He said they have great programs for that stuff. I'll connect you guys if you want."

Megan laughed, "Great, but just know I'm done dating your friends after this summer."

I chuckled back, "It is close to Dartmouth if you ever wanna, you know, hang out sometime."

Megan gripped my hand gently and nodded. "I'd like that."

My parents emerged from the church and I looked back at Megan.

"I better be going," I said. "Don't want to get in the habit of tardiness."

Megan LaMarre shook her head and adjusted her Ray Bans.

"No, you do not," she smirked.

***

After my bags were packed, I went on one final jog through Bayside, content to relish in the late-summer peace that was soon to envelop the region. Once I passed the golf club, I made a turn toward the Jackson residence, still expecting to see the for-sale sign in the yard. Word usually spread like wildfire when a listing went up around here, but I worried the recent events had scared off usual prospects, let alone at the Jackson house of all places.

As I approached the yard, I heard the sound of a lawnmower. I stopped and waited for the rider to appear from behind the house, where I recognized Steve Hamilton on the seat. I suppose he had been the one to take care of the landscaping while it was being sold, perhaps a posthumous favor to an old pal. Steve spotted me on the road and cut the engine.

"Hey Billy!" he called, walking over and taking off his gloves. He reached me and we shook hands.

"Hey, Steve," I said back, nodding around at the work he had done. "Looks great."

"Thanks bud. Almost done, thank God. I'm too old for this shit. Just ask your dad, he'll agree."

I laughed, "Looks like a great retirement gig though."

Steve rolled his eyes.

I started to ask him about the Patriots opening game next week but he cut me off before I could get the full words out.

"So your buddy got a promotion, eh?" Steve asked, raising his eyebrow.

"Uh, which one?" I replied. Nothing came to mind.

"You know," Steve made a quick scan of the yard. "The fed we both worked with. He's gonna be the task force director now."

I paused, the only one I could think of was Sam.

"Wells? How do you know him?" I asked.

"Billy," Steve smirked. "Who do you think told Wells that Mr. Jackson was in trouble with those cats?"

At last, it occurred to me. Sam always mentioned that he had another source but he never ended up telling me, likely out of safety and protection. Steve Hamilton was that guy. Out of years of friendship, Steve was the only other one to get close enough to earn Myles' trust. Steve never spoke a word to anyone until he feared for his friend's safety. That's when Sam must've been informed.

"Wow," I shook my head. "That's incredible. How'd you know Wells?"

"His pops and my buddy ran a fishing charter in Marblehead. Saw Sammy and his old block once a year when he was a tike. Sammy grew up, and I followed along. Can't never hurt to have friends in high places!"

"Are you, uh, all good now though Mr. Hamilton?"

"Oh yeah, I'm good. All safe and sound. I'll be taking my ketch to Florida come October and Belfast will just be my summer port."

"You're not worried about getting harassed or chased by anyone?" I asked.

"No way, Billy," he scoffed, scratching his head and removing his safety glasses. "If the highest aim of a captain were to preserve his ship, he would leave it in port forever."

I chuckled. "That's a good one. 'You come up with that?"

"No, not me. Saint Augustine or something. But write it down anyway."

We both laughed again and I reached out to shake his hand again, thankful for his words of wisdom, his conviction, and his moral clarity. This place, and the world, despite all of its recent failures, was home to good people and good ideals. For that, we are all better off.

I waved goodbye to Mr. Hamilton as I jogged back toward home, realizing it was getting dark and that I had a long drive ahead of me in the morning. A clearing between the trees emerged, where the moon's shadow was beginning to reveal itself over the water.

When I was younger, I learned that the moon moved the tides and that without tides, the balance of our planet would be forever disrupted, and as a result, impossible to inhabit. The explanation for how something as far away as the moon could have that big of an impact was simple to an eight-year-old. Because Gravity.

And yet, that explanation, perhaps both simple and yet still beyond what I am supposed to comprehend, rings true. I may never be able to explain, without some sort of divine providence, what led me to witness and shape these events in Bayside. But it's possible that just as the moon is tied to the earth for the sake of balance, my friends, family, and I were tied to Myles Jackson to help balance our little world.

Epilogue

My campus mailbox was stuffed and my Instagram direct messages were overflowing. I was so sick of people trying to get their scoop, even four months after the arrests back home in Maine. I had only agreed to talk to one journalist during the Winter break, someone I trusted who used to cover my hockey games and was now a news reporter. No one else was going to break my wall.

I shuffled upstairs to my apartment, overlooking East Wheelock Street. A Dartmouth Big Green flag hung in our foyer. Outside our windows, holiday lights were slowly beginning to line the houses and buildings in Hanover. Soon a parade of Audis and Lexuses would descend upon the town, and shortly thereafter depart back to their origins for Thanksgiving. We wouldn't return until the new year, which would be my last semester at Dartmouth.

An L.L. Bean puffer jacket hung from my bureau. I hadn't used it to retrieve my mail, despite how chilly it was becoming in the hills of New Hampshire. An afternoon sea breeze had been traded this fall for a crisp morning chill. The trees were bare. A stray brown leaf stuck to my shoe, and I flicked it off as I sat down on the prized black futon that glorified our otherwise stuffy flat.

The first piece of mail was a reminder that I still had time to take the LSATs again before the next round of applications was due. I tossed it aside, happy that it wasn't a campaign mailer anymore.

Soon, I saw an orange envelope addressed to me from New London, only a short drive down the highway. It was from Megan, fully enjoying her time at Colby-Sawyer College. Upon opening it, the card wished me and my family a happy Thanksgiving and displayed a reel of photos we had taken at an orchard several weeks prior. My favorite one included me holding a pumpkin while Megan tugged on my flannel as if to drag me into a pile of leaves. I smiled seeing that again.

Our relationship wasn't official, and it certainly was still very casual and platonic, yet I felt over time it could still progress to something more significant. After all, there were a lot of leftover feelings from the summer. The initial flame had re-ignited after Megan's visit outside the church. No matter what happened, I appreciated how Megan wrote to me, even if she didn't need to. I stuck the photo reel inside a nearby textbook for safekeeping. There was no need to risk my suitemates asking prying questions.

The last piece of mail came from an unlikely source. A postcard - not from my folks in Maine like usual - this time from a much sunnier place. The edges had started to bend, but you could still easily see the huge palm grove and white sand beach pictured prominently. ***PARADISE ISLAND***, it read in bright tropical colors. I smiled and flipped it over.

Dear Billy,

Hope you're enjoying your last year at the real Dartmouth. Come visit me sometime, I found something you might be interested in seeing. Happy Holidays to you and your family.

- *Steve Hamilton*

A small part of me wishes the postcard had been from Uncle Jack. However, a vague and ambiguous invitation from Mr. Hamilton also sparked my curiosity after what he revealed to me before I went back to school. I studied the postcard for a moment and later set it next to the photos from Megan.

For another time, I thought. *For another time.*

Acknowledgments

Anyone who has ever completed a voluminous project knows that it is often filled with unforeseen challenges. Thankfully, my obstacles have been overcome because of the tremendous support I have received in this endeavor. Therefore, this book is not only a product of my writing, but also answered prayer, encouraging words from others, and widespread enthusiasm received to date. Without such support, I likely wouldn't have kept going.

At the age of twelve, I tried to write a novel but to no surprise never saw it through. Thankfully over the past fifteen years, countless teachers and professors have helped me refine my skills to a point where I felt confident to try again. Similarly, various editors, many of whom I still have never met in person, granted me opportunities to publish my sports articles and receive meaningful feedback. To this date, I am grateful for them all.

My friends and colleagues - including other accomplished writers - have also cheered me on from the sidelines. Often, I worried that nobody would find my pursuit of completion interesting, but many of them frequently asked for updates once word got out that I was writing *Bayside*. Maybe they do think I am cool.

And of course, God blessed me with an incredible family. From the beginning, my parents, siblings, in-laws, aunts, uncles, and cousins who knew of my work encouraged me and congratulated me, often before anything substantial was even written. I love them all. The support of my wife, Summer, was second to none. She is my best friend.

Thank you for helping me make *Bayside* a reality. More to come.

About the Author

William H. Hyland is a Searsmont, Maine native and a graduate of Colby-Sawyer College in New London, New Hampshire. His other nonfiction work has been found in the *Pen Bay Pilot, Yawkey Way Report*, the *Bangor Daily News* and in publications of the Society for American Baseball Research. William now resides in Lisbon, Maine with his wife Summer. *Bayside* is his first novel.

Made in the USA
Middletown, DE
20 December 2024